It almost [...]
to see hi[...]
for her, and she wanted to take
his hand, put her arms around
him and tell him that she
understood. That one day it
would be all right.

"Please, don't feel like you have to laugh," she said. "It isn't in the least bit compulsory."

"Okay." And without warning, deep lines fanned out from his eyes and the smile became the real thing.

Kay had to catch her breath and force herself to concentrate on the job at hand. Dominic Ravenscar did it for her.

"What happened to your daughter's father?"

The abrupt change of subject threw her, and she responded to this unexpected jab at a raw nerve in much the same way as he had. Instinctively. Defensively.

"Polly never had a father."

Dear Reader,

Several of my books have touched on the lives of the inhabitants of Upper Haughton. Willow and Mike Armstrong from *The Runaway Bride* settled here. The Hilliards from *A Perfect Proposal* live in the Old Rectory. Jake and Amy Hallam, from my RITA®-nominated book, *The Bachelor's Baby*, live here, too. They've moved out of Amy's cottage and bought a larger house for their growing family, but Old Cottage isn't empty. Kay Lovell—who works at the village shop, makes prize-winning marmalade and spends all her spare time helping out the neighbors—lives there with her daughter, Polly.

Linden Lodge, however, has stood empty for six years. The garden is running wild, the blackberries are tempting—and desperately needed for the village harvest supper—and the lock on the gate is broken. But Kay's trespass doesn't go unnoticed....

Upper Haughton is a real village; a place from my own childhood. I've only changed the name. Come and visit.

Warmest wishes,

Liz

A FAMILY OF HIS OWN

Liz Fielding

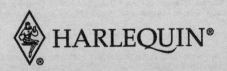

HARLEQUIN®

TORONTO • NEW YORK • LONDON
AMSTERDAM • PARIS • SYDNEY • HAMBURG
STOCKHOLM • ATHENS • TOKYO • MILAN • MADRID
PRAGUE • WARSAW • BUDAPEST • AUCKLAND

ISBN 0-373-03798-8

A FAMILY OF HIS OWN

First North American Publication 2004.

Copyright © 2004 by Liz Fielding.

PROLOGUE

'SHE'S so beautiful, Jake.' Amy Hallam gently touched the cheek of the newborn infant, then lifted her from the cradle and tucked her into the crook of her shoulder, breathing in the baby scent as she kissed the top of her downy head. 'Her mother just left her on Aunt Lucy's doorstep? The poor woman must have been distraught...'

'Distraught maybe, but she knew Lucy would take care of her. She left a note.' Jake handed his wife a sheet of paper and then took the baby from her so that she could read it.

Amy flinched as she touched the scrap of paper, physically sensing the emotional turmoil, the very real fear of the woman who'd written it.

'Are you all right?' Jake put out a hand to steady her.

'Fine,' she said, her mouth dry. But she sat down before she began to read.

Dear "Aunt Lucy"

You took care of me once and now I'm asking you to take care of my baby because there's no one else I can turn to.

She was born on the 26th September. She has no name—if I don't know her name I can't betray her— and her birth has not been registered. She is totally anonymous. It is her only hope.

I'm begging you, trusting you, not to tell the au-

5

thorities about her, not to make any appeals through the media for me to come forward. That will only draw attention to her, put her in danger.

I'm leaving what little money I have to help you until you can find some good people to take her in, give her a good life. I love her, but she isn't safe with me.

K.

Amy blinked, focusing on the shimmering image of her own infant son as he scooted around on his bottom, irrationally wanting to grab him close, just to let him know how much she loved him. Instead she reached out wordlessly, and clasped her husband's hand.

'Paranoia? Domestic violence?' he asked, trusting her instincts.

'I don't know, but this woman is terrified of something.' Then, 'You've only got to look at the handwriting,' she said quickly as Jake quirked a brow at her, taken aback at her instant response. 'Whatever the problem is, she's beyond reason. She must know what she asks is impossible, that it breaks every childcare law in the book, but her only thought is to hide the baby.'

'We can't do that for long.'

'No, of course not. But I'm not prepared to take any unnecessary risks. A week or two will make no difference.'

'I'm not sure that the social services will see it that way.'

'Maybe not, but if we could find her...'

'She's placed her infant in what she believes is a safe haven, Amy. Surely she's going to put as much distance between them as she can?'

'Not until she's sure. She'll stay close until she's certain her baby is safe.'

'How will that help? We have no idea what she looks like.'

She frowned. 'Maybe we don't need to. She's left all her money with Lucy. She'll be weak. Hungry. In a pretty bad way. We need to search the lanes around Lucy's cottage, Jake. There's no time to lose.'

CHAPTER ONE

"If reasons were as plentiful as blackberries..."
William Shakespeare

It was hot for the end of September. A cloudless, still day with only the blackberries to warn that summer was almost over.

Huge glistening fruit that was infuriatingly out of reach.

Kay rubbed the sweat from her forehead, fanned herself with her tattered straw gardening hat and walked slowly back along the hedge, seeking out any that she'd missed, trying to ignore the long brambles lolling over the high wall that skirted the far side of the lane. Brambles weighed down by berries, but which still just evaded the reach of her walking stick.

'Come on, Polly, this will have to do,' she said, after scanning the hedge one last time.

'Have you got **en**ough?' her daughter asked, looking doubtfully at the pitiful quantity they'd gathered.

'There aren't any more. I'm afraid the harvest-supper pies will have to be more apple than blackberry this year.'

Polly's little face wrinkled up in a frown. 'But there are loads up there,' she said, pointing at the top of the wall.

'I know, poppet, but I can't reach them.'

'You could get them down from the other side. Why

8

don't you go through the gate? No one lives there. Someone's put up a For Sale sign,' she added, as if that settled the matter.

How simple life was when you were six years old! But Polly was right about one thing. Linden Lodge had been empty for as long as she'd lived in Upper Haughton.

From her bedroom window she had tantalising glimpses of the wilderness hidden behind the high walls. The roof of an ornamental summer house collapsing beneath the unrestrained vigour of a *Clematis montana*. Roses running wild. Blossom on trees where, year after year, the ripened fruit had been left to fall and rot in the grass. It was like a secret garden from a fairy tale, locked away, hidden, sleeping. Just waiting for the right person to venture inside, bring it back to life.

It would take more than a kiss, she thought.

When she didn't answer, Polly, with all the persistence of a six-year-old on a mission, said, 'They're for the *harvest supper*.'

'What?'

Polly gave a huge sigh. 'The *blackberries*, of course. Everyone in the village is supposed to give something.'

'Oh, yes.' That was the plan. Everyone contributed to the harvest supper that brought the whole village together in a celebration of the year; a tradition linking them back to the agricultural past of the village.

Her reluctance to try the gate was ridiculous, she knew. If she didn't pick it the fruit would just shrivel up. Which would be a wicked waste.

'You could put a note through the door to say thank you,' Polly said.

Kay found herself smiling. 'A thank-you note? Who to?'

'Whoever buys the house. And I'll draw a picture of the pies so that when they move in they'll be happy that their blackberries didn't go to waste,' she said, tugging impatiently at her hand and leading her towards the gate. It wasn't actually a gate, as such, but a gardener's door set into the wall, the faded green paint cracking and peeling in the afternoon sun, neglected as the garden.

'It'll be locked,' she said. Of course it would be locked.

Reason might suggest that she was doing the right thing but as she gripped the handle—her heart beating rather faster than normal—turned it and gave it a push, it still felt like trespassing. There was some initial resistance but then, just as she was about to back off with feelings that were a confused mixture of relief and disappointment, it shifted suddenly and flew back until it was stopped by the weeds.

A blackbird, pinking crossly at the disturbance, flew up out of the long grass, startling her, and she froze, half expecting to hear an angry voice demanding to know what the devil she thought she was doing.

It was just her conscience having its say.

Apart from the sound of her heartbeat hammering away in her ears, only the murmurous hum of bees busily working the vivid clumps of old-fashioned late-summer perennials, stockpiling their larders against the long winter, disturbed the silence.

Blue and purple Michaelmas daisies, *Rudbeckia*, *Sedum*. The tough species, survivors that could fight their corner against the rank weeds that had invaded the borders.

It cried out to her gardener's heart to see someone's hard work abandoned to the ravages of nature, and nothing could now have stopped her from putting her shoulder to the gate, forcing it back against the weeds and grass that had grown against it, to take a closer look.

Dominic Ravenscar turned his back on the drawing room, the ghostly shapes of furniture hidden beneath dust covers, and stared out at the neglected garden.

It was the moment he'd most dreaded, one he'd been running from for six years, this first sight of Sara's garden. But no matter how hard he'd run, the demons had kept pace with him until he'd finally understood that there was no place far enough to escape the pain, no shadows deep enough to hide from his memories.

The last time he'd looked through the French windows it had been late spring. The fruit trees had been in blossom, the buds were thickening in the lilac, clumps of yellow tulips were spilling their petals over the grass and Sara had been blooming too with the glow of the new life they'd created. It had still been their secret, a private joy to be hugged to themselves for a while before they shared the news once the first uncertain weeks were safely past.

A double tragedy he had kept to himself, too. After her death it had been too late to share the joy and there had been pain enough to go around without making the aching loss even harder to bear for family and friends.

This vaster emptiness was his alone.

A lax stem from the rose she'd planted to grow "around the door" tapped against the French windows, startling him, forcing him to focus on the present. It wasn't the only thing that had run wild.

Without Sara to tend it, care for it, nature had been quick to move in and take over. Shrubs were pressing towards the house, lank and overgrown, squeezing out the perennials that were fighting a losing battle for light and air. Weeds had colonised the cracks in the stone paving and grass had grown over the stepping-stone path that curved down beyond the summer house in the direction of the kitchen garden—even that was being crushed under the weight of some climber—while beyond it he glimpsed invasive brambles scrambling unchecked over the fruit trees she'd trained against the wall.

He rested his forehead against the warm glass, closed his eyes to shut out the wreck of his garden, the wreck of his life, but his mind wouldn't let him rest. He'd bought the house because she'd fallen in love with this garden, enclosed as it was within high walls of old, rose-coloured brick. It would be a safe place, she'd said, for their children to play.

She'd become passionate about making an old-fashioned English garden, crammed with native plants that would attract butterflies and birds. In his mind's eye he could see her now, ignoring the rain as she set about her roses with the secateurs, catch glimpses of her with her straw hat jammed on her head to protect her fair skin from the sun as she tied the young branches of the peach tree back against the far wall to enhance the kitchen garden.

Walking amongst the fruit trees of the small orchard she'd planted.

There was no escape from the pain in darkness and he opened his eyes. And still he saw her, pulling down the brambles as if admonishing his neglect...

'Sara…'

His mouth moved but no sound emerged, only the thudding of his heart swelling and pounding in his throat. Then he was wrenching at the door, desperate to get to her. It refused to budge and it took a moment for him to realise that it was locked, that the keys were on the kitchen table where he'd thrown them. Out of reach. Because he dared not move, dared not turn away for a second. If he took his eyes off her she'd disappear…

Instead he hammered desperately at the glass with his bunched fists, wanting her to turn around and look at him.

If she looked, if she saw him too, everything would be all right…

'Sara!'

'Dom, are you OK?'

Momentarily distracted, he blinked, half turned…and when he looked back she'd gone.

'Dom?'

At first it had happened all the time. Everywhere he'd looked he'd thought he saw her. A glimpse of long, sun-streaked blonde hair in a crowd, a ripple of laughter in a restaurant, a flash of her favourite colour had been enough to stop his heart. It had been a long time since the experience had been so vivid, so real…

Since it had left him feeling quite so bleak. Quite so alone.

'I'm fine, Greg,' he said abruptly, turning away from the window and realising that he was the object of very real concern. It was an expression he'd come to know well in the months after Sara's death. One of the reasons he'd gone away, choosing to keep on the move, live and work amongst strangers who didn't know anything about him. Didn't know what had happened. People who didn't have to hunt for words because they didn't know what to say. People who, after their initial friendly overtures were rejected, backed off and kept their distance. 'I'm fine.'

'There's no need to put yourself through this, you know,' Greg said, putting down the box of groceries he'd fetched from the car. 'You could leave everything to me. Just tell me what you want to keep and I'll get it packed up, put in store for you until you…well, until you need it.' Then, more brightly, 'It won't take long to sell the house. You could sell a garden shed in Upper Haughton. It was an astute investment…'

'I didn't buy it as an investment. I bought it because—'

'I know,' he cut in quickly. 'I'm sorry.'

He shook his head. He knew Greg was just talking to fill the silence.

'Look, why don't you just come and stay with us until it's sorted?'

'No.' Then, perceiving that he had been abrupt, knowing that Greg deserved better, he said, 'Thank you, but there are things I need to go through. I should have done it a long time ago.' He turned back to the window, hoping against hope that she'd be there again, but the garden was empty.

'Right.' There was a pause, then, following his glance out of the window, 'Do you need some help to sort through…things? It doesn't have to be anyone you know. I could ask the agency who supplies us with staff if they have someone. It might be easier with someone who isn't emotionally, well, you know…'

He knew, but he didn't want help. He didn't want

anyone. He just wanted Greg to stop looking at him as if he was losing it and instead go away and leave him alone. But the man wasn't just his lawyer, he was the friend who'd stood at his side as he promised to be faithful to Sara until death parted them. Meaningless words. They were young. In love. They were going to live forever...

'Thank you, Greg,' he said, taking pity on him, knowing that he just wanted to help but didn't know how, impotent in the face of such unimaginable grief. 'Can I let you know?'

'Of course.' Then, 'Are you sure you're going to be all right here?' he said, looking around. 'If you'd given me a bit of warning, I could have got someone in to give the place a thorough going over. Your once-a-month people haven't been doing more than the minimum by the looks of things.'

'That's all I paid them to do.' The minimum. He'd told them not to disturb anything. 'I've got water and power. A cellphone. It's all I need.'

'What about some transport?'

'I'm not going anywhere.'

'Right,' he said after a long pause, during which he'd clearly debated whether it would be safe to leave him. 'I'll be off, then.' Receiving no encouragement to stay, he continued, 'If you're sure? That box of groceries is pretty basic.'

'Don't worry. I've managed to keep body and soul together for six years. I'm not about to starve myself to death.'

Greg looked as if he was about to say something, but thought better of it. He didn't need to say anything. Dom had seen the shocked look he hadn't been quite swift enough to hide when he'd picked him up at the airport.

He turned back to look once more at the garden and his heart lifted a beat. She was there again, her hat shading her face as she looked around as if seeking something she'd lost. Tall, slender in a pair of baggy denim jeans, a faded turquoise T-shirt. It had always been her favourite colour.

'I'll call you tomorrow,' Greg said from the door. 'We'll talk about some help.'

'No rush,' he said absently, willing her to look up— look at him. Then he was distracted by another movement as a little girl leapt up out of the grass, holding up a loop of flowers. A daisy chain of some kind. Sara put it on the child's head so that she looked like a little princess.

He was sure she was laughing. If only he could see her face.

'No rush...' he said again as the door clicked shut. Hands pressed against the glass, he watched as, having bent to kiss the child, she reached into her back pocket, took out a pair of secateurs and reached down to cut through the thick stem of the brambles. 'I've got all the time in the world.'

Then he saw that she wasn't wearing gloves.

He'd bought her a pair, but she always tore them off, impatient with her clumsiness in the thick, thorn-proof protection.

As he watched, a bramble whipped back and caught her hand.

'No...'

She eased it carefully from her skin, then put her

thumb to her mouth, sucked it, and, like a recurring nightmare, history began to repeat itself…

'Sara…'

But her name choked in his throat and he slid down the glass as the image shimmered, then shattered as he slammed his lids shut.

'Heavens, Kay, you've done well.' Amy Hallam placed a bowl with a few blackberries in it on the kitchen table. 'I thought I'd help out, but there really isn't much fruit in our paddock. The goat nibbles any bramble shoots the minute they appear.'

'Goats eat anything the minute it appears above ground.' Kay rinsed the fruit and added it to the pan simmering on the stove. 'But thanks for the thought. I'm afraid I had to do something rather bad to ensure that the blackberry and apple pies weren't just apple this year.'

'Bad? You? How unexpected.' She grinned. 'How promising.'

'Stop it. I'm serious. I raided the garden at Linden Lodge. Egged on, I have to tell you, by your god-daughter.'

'What's bad about that? It would have been a crime to let them go to waste. Polly's a bright child and I've done my godmotherly duty in teaching her to use her initiative.'

'The resident blackbird didn't take your relaxed view—'

'Let him eat worms.'

'—and I broke the latch on the gate when I pushed it open.'

'Scrumping and vandalism in one fell swoop,' Amy

said with a grin. 'You're a one-woman crime wave, Kay Lovell. The neighbourhood-watch coordinator will have to be informed. Oh, wait. You are the neighbourhood-watch coordinator—'

'Oh, stop it,' Kay said, unable to suppress her answering grin. Then, picking up the kettle, 'Coffee?'

'Please. Do you want me to send someone over to fix the gate?'

'No, I can handle it. The bit that the bolt slides into had rusted away, that's all. I'm sure I've got one in the shed.'

'What's it like in there?'

'The shed? Do you want to do a landlady's inspection now? I really should have some notice so that I can tidy up a bit...'

'Linden Lodge.'

Yes, well, she knew that was what Amy meant. She wasn't sure she wanted to talk about it though.

'It's so mysterious behind those high walls,' Amy prompted.

'No, just overgrown,' Kay said. 'Polly sat down to make a Michaelmas-daisy chain while I cut back the brambles and she completely disappeared. Just for a minute I thought...' She let it go. She didn't want to remember how she'd felt in those few horrible seconds when Polly had failed to respond to her call. When all she could see was the open gate and a million hideous possibilities had rushed into her head...

'You cut back the brambles?' Amy asked, distracting her.

'What? Oh, well, yes. They were strangling an espaliered peach. Poor thing.' She concentrated on spooning coffee into the cafetière. 'Don't snigger, Amy.'

'Me? Snigger? Perish the thought.'

'Well, don't smile, then. I know it was pathetic of me. I just can't bear to see anything suffering.' She stopped, turned away to take down a couple of mugs. She knew she didn't have to explain. Amy never needed explanations. She just seemed to know. 'Anyway,' she said, 'I'll drop a note through the letterbox tomorrow when I go and fix the gate. Just to explain.'

'About cutting back the brambles to save the peach tree?'

'About nicking the blackberries. For a good cause.'

'There's no one at home to care and ghosts don't need explanations, Kay.'

Startled, she turned to look at her visitor. 'Ghosts?'

'You didn't feel it? The garden always feels haunted to me whenever I walk past.'

'No. It wasn't creepy, just…sad.'

'Maybe that's what I meant.'

Kay didn't think so. She hadn't felt any ghosts there, but Amy was well known locally for her slightly fey qualities, her ability to feel more than most people could see.

'A For Sale board went up on Friday. Did you know?' she said, determined to change the subject. She hadn't felt anything beyond sadness, yet even now her skin was goosing. And she had to go back there to fix the gate.

'I heard it was on the market. Such a pity.'

'Did you know the people who lived there?'

'The Ravenscars? Not well. We'd met at village events, of course—the fête, a fundraiser for the hall, that sort of thing—but I was busy with the children. I had Mark that year and I was still establishing the business. They were younger, hadn't been married more than a year or two and were still more interested in each other than anyone else. They came to the harvest supper, though. I remember Sara Ravenscar was thrilled at the way the whole village comes together for that. She'd have approved of you having the blackberries.' Then, 'Her death was such a tragedy.'

'I heard she died from tetanus poisoning. Is that true?'

'Well there were complications, but can you believe it in this day and age! Apparently her parents didn't believe in any kind of vaccination and, like most enthusiastic gardeners, she couldn't keep a pair of gloves on.' Then, 'After she died Dominic went overseas. I heard he was working on some kind of aid programme.'

'I'm surprised he didn't sell the house, or let it. Rather than let it stand empty. Whoever buys it will need to put in a lot of work and not just in the garden. The paintwork is in a very poor state.'

'Maybe he couldn't bear to let it go so soon. Then I suppose coming back seemed even worse so he shut it out. Now he's like a needle stuck in an old gramophone record, unable to move on.'

Kay gave a little shiver, as if a goose had walked over her grave. 'Well, he's put it on the market now. That's movement of a sort.'

'Maybe. I hope so.'

'Yes, well, I'll take the wheelbarrow and clear up the stuff I chopped down when I fix the gate. Maybe I should approach the agents and see if they want the garden properly tidied up. I've rather let my own business slide while Polly has been off school for the summer.'

Amy looked as if she was about to say something, but when she hesitated and Kay raised her brows she just said, 'Bearing in mind what happened to Sara Ravenscar, make sure you wear gloves. Have you put something on those scratches?'

'Tea-tree oil.' She glanced at her hand where the sharp thorns had caught her when one of the brambles had whipped back suddenly. 'The minute I got home. And my shots are up-to-date.'

'Good.' Then, as a pyjama-clad Polly hurtled into the room, Amy turned to scoop her up into her arms. 'Hey, sweetheart! Just the girl I wanted to see. Can your mummy spare you tomorrow?'

Polly, who knew when a treat was being offered, still hesitated. 'Tomorrow?'

'All day. We're taking the boys to the sea and Mark really, really wants you to come too.'

Her eyes went round. 'Oh, wicked!' Then, 'But I've promised to help Mummy make the pies…'

'I think I can manage,' Kay assured her, trying hard to ignore the stab of annoyance that Amy had left her with no real choice. 'If Amy can,' she added. 'Are you quite sure you can cope?'

'Absolutely. Four children works better than three. Jake can do adventurous things with George and James and I get to have fun rootling around the rock pools with the little ones.'

And the unspoken message that she needed to let Polly go sometimes, that being quite so protective was not good for either of them, came across loud and clear.

'Well, in that case, how can I resist? I hope you all have a lovely day.'

'Did you see how many blackberries we picked, Amy?' Polly demanded, snapping the tension that stretched between them. 'And I made a purple daisy chain, too.'

'Purple? You're kidding me!'

'No, honestly! Come and see...' She wriggled free and, grabbing Amy's hand, tugged her towards the stairs.

'I'll be right back.'

'I won't hold my breath,' Kay responded, flipping the off switch on the kettle. 'Just don't let her sandbag you into telling her another story. You've got children of your own to put to bed.'

'Yes, but they're all boys. They don't do fairies. Or daisy chains. Besides, Jake's on bathroom-and-story duty tonight and I have no intention of returning until he's mopped up the mess.'

Dom forced himself to heat up a can of soup, eat some bread. Tasting nothing, but going through the motions of living as he had done every day for the last six years. Yet for the first time in as long as he could remember, he was aware of his heart beating.

Afterwards he walked through the house, touching the things that lay undisturbed on Sara's dressing table, coated with the thin layer of dust that had settled since the cleaners' last visit. Opening the cupboards where her clothes still hung, lifting the soft material of a dress he remembered her wearing, rubbing it against his cheek.

Her scent lingered and he breathed it in.

How stupid he'd been. She was here. All the time he'd been running, Sara had been here, waiting for him.

Downstairs he unlocked the French windows and opened them wide. He didn't venture beyond the paved area where they'd sat together on sunny evenings with a glass of wine, half-afraid he'd disturb her presence as she lingered in the garden. Half hoping that she'd walk out of the gathering dusk to join him.

But the garden remained still and silent. Even this late in the summer the heat clung to the walls, filling the air with the scent of late roses, and for a while he sat there, every cell focused on the wilderness that had once been a garden, hoping for one more glimpse of her before it grew too dark to see.

Then the sound of childish laughter floated towards him and instead of cutting him to the quick as it usually did, a poignant reminder of everything he'd lost, he found himself leaning towards it, straining to hear more. Holding his breath. Not moving while the sky darkened to the deepest blue and the first stars began to appear.

He didn't move until it was quite dark and nothing was visible within the deep shadows of the walled garden.

CHAPTER TWO

"There has fallen a splendid tear
From the passion-flower at the gate.
She is coming, my dove, my dear;
She is coming, my life, my fate."

Alfred, Lord Tennyson

KAY DIDN'T waste any time. The minute she'd waved Polly goodbye, she loaded up her wheelbarrow with the tools she'd need and headed for Linden Lodge. She'd behaved embarrassingly out of character yesterday and she wanted this over and done with.

She did her bit for the community, helped in the village school, worked hard to support herself and Polly, and she kept her head down. She never stepped out of line, never did anything to attract attention to herself, cause talk. There'd been enough of that to last a lifetime when Amy had first taken them under her wing, then let them move into the cottage.

She couldn't think what had possessed her.

She stopped, parked the barrow.

She was lying to herself. She knew exactly what had possessed her.

The mystery of a garden locked away from view. That was what had possessed her. A chance to see more than the tantalising glimpses of it she could see from her upstairs windows. She'd wanted to see more. She'd always wanted to see more.

Polly wouldn't have talked her into trespassing unless she'd been a willing accomplice.

As she pushed back the gate, the mingled scents of crushed grass, germander, valerian gone to seed everywhere, welcomed her. The blackbird, perched in an old apple tree, paused momentarily in his song and then continued. And she felt...accepted.

What utter nonsense.

She set about the grass and weeds behind the gate, making short work of them with her shears, so that she could open it wide enough to manoeuvre her big wheelbarrow inside.

Then, since securing the gate was more important than tidying up some mess no one was likely to see in the very near future—and she *was* the neighbourhood-watch coordinator—the first thing she did was to replace the bolt. She oiled the hinges, too. It was the neighbourly thing to do and little enough thanks for all the blackberries.

As if anyone would notice. The buyers—and there would be buyers; no one was going to be put off by tired paintwork, a neglected garden...it was rare for a house in Upper Haughton to come on to the market—wouldn't give a hoot. They'd probably rip it out and replace it with a fancy new one. Which was a shame. The old one, despite the cracked and peeling paint—where paint still remained—had character.

They would probably grub out the high-maintenance cottage garden, too, and replace it with something modern that wouldn't involve a constant battle with slugs, blackspot on the roses, the rust that attacked the old-fashioned hollyhocks if they weren't constantly watched.

They'd certainly tear down the crumbling summer house.

Maybe they'd put in a swimming pool.

She tossed the oil can into the barrow and looked around. It was still early, quiet as only a village that didn't lead to anywhere else, tucked away from the main road, could be on a Sunday morning.

Tattered dew-laced spider webs sparkled in the low, slanting sunlight, slender crimson berries of the *Berberis thunbergii* glistened like droplets of blood against purple leaves that were fading to autumn crimson, and in the little orchard ripe apples were poised in that moment of perfection before they fell to the grass to be plundered by birds and hedgehogs and wasps before the insects and micro-organisms got to work and they rotted away to nothing. The food chain in action.

She walked the overgrown paths, sighing over the horticultural treasures that were struggling to survive against the more robust species. The temptation was to linger, set them free. But what would be the point? Without continuous care nature would rampage into the vacuum she created with renewed vigour. She'd do more harm than good.

She hadn't needed Amy Hallam's raised eyebrows to know that wasting her time cutting back the brambles had been plain stupid. In the spring they'd be back, stronger than ever, and in the meantime she was having to pay for her ridiculous gesture with time and effort that would have been better spent on her own garden.

She certainly didn't have time to waste daydreaming about how this one would look if it was rescued from neglect, she reminded herself, and pulled on thick leather gloves before she set to work chopping up the brambles so that they'd fit into her barrow.

And did her very best to ignore the delicate branches of a witch hazel that was being strangled by bindweed.

Dom started awake and for a moment he had no idea where he was. Knew only that he was cold and stiff from a night spent in an armchair. That at least was a familiar experience.

He rubbed his hands over his face, dragged his fingers through his hair, eased his limbs as he willed himself to face another day. Then, as he sat forward, he saw the garden, sparkling as the sunlight caught the dew.

For a moment it looked like a magical place.

And then, as he caught a glimpse of Sara at work near the summer house, he knew it was. No longer feeling the ache in his limbs, or in his heart, he stood up and walked down the shallow steps into the garden, oblivious to the wet grass soaking his feet.

All that he cared about was that his beloved Sara was here, working in her garden, kneeling in front of a small shrub, gently releasing it from the stranglehold of some weed. And he was going to help her.

Engrossed in her task, taking care not to snap the slender branches of the shrub as she unravelled the bindweed, Kay had scarcely any warning that she wasn't alone.

Only the rustle of grass that she assumed was a bird, or one of the squirrels which, having already come to give her the once-over and decided she was harmless, had continued their own busy harvest of the hazel copse on the far side of the wall.

Nothing more.

Scarcely a moment to register the presence beside her, a heartbeat for fear to seize her before he was on his knees beside her.

'Sara…'

His voice shivered through her, held her.

Sara?

The word was spoken soft and low, as if to a nervous colt that might shy away, bolt at the least excuse.

Maybe she had started because, more urgently, he said, 'Don't go…'

Soft, low, it was a heartbreaking appeal and she needed no introduction to know that this gaunt, hollow-eyed man was Dominic Ravenscar. Needed none of Amy's famed insight to make the leap from his low plea to an understanding that, with her back to the sun, her face shadowed by the broad brim of her hat, he thought she was his poor dead wife come back to him.

Needed no feminine intuition to know that whatever she did was going to be wrong. Was going to hurt him. Even as she struggled to find the words, he said, 'I won't leave you again. Ever.'

She remained frozen in the act of slicing through the bindweed, unable to think, unable to move.

There were no words.

While she knelt there, trying to decide what to do, he reached out and, as if it was the most natural thing in the world, began to unravel the bindweed she'd cut through. As his hand brushed against hers a jolt, like the discharge of static electricity, shot through her and she dropped the pocket knife.

As if afraid that she would disappear, he caught her hand, held it for a moment. His fingers were long and wrapped around her own hand with ease. His hand and wrist were deeply tanned, strong, attenuated like those of a fasting saint in some medieval painting.

He traced the scratch on the back of her hand where the bramble had caught her with his thumb.

'You aren't wearing gloves,' he said. 'How many times have I told you that you should wear gloves?'

'No… Yes…' She mouthed the words, but her voice, thick with the choking rush of emotional overload, didn't make it past her throat.

Maybe he heard her anyway, or maybe he just read her lips. Maybe he thought she was making him a promise instead of desperately searching for the words to tell him, make him see that she was someone else, because he reached out with his other hand, cupping her face in his long palm. And while she remained locked between the need to run and the certainty that she must stay and convince him of the reality of the situation, he leaned forward and kissed her.

It had been a lifetime since she'd been kissed and never with this sweetness, this gentleness. As if she was something precious but fragile that might shatter to dust if he was careless.

Her body, starved of tenderness, starved of the touch of a man, responded like a primrose to the sun after a long, hard winter, and, overriding her brain, she returned the kiss with every scrap of longing, all the need engendered by years of emptiness.

The kiss deepened as his confidence grew that she would not vanish at his touch.

Her hat fell to the grass as his fingers slid through her hair and he cradled her head as it fell back beneath the sweet invasion of his mouth.

The stubble on his unshaven jaw rasped against her

face. His hand curved about her waist, drawing her into a closer embrace, crushing her against him as if he would make them one. In the tree above them, the blackbird pinked an urgent warning. And she felt his hot tears against her cheek. Or maybe they were her own.

The kiss had a dream-like quality, the perfection of fantasy, and it seemed that a lifetime had passed before his hold on her eased and he straightened. While her breathing returned to something approaching normality.

An age while he looked down into her face, confronted reality, and his expression of perfect joy turned first to confusion, then to pain as he realised his mistake.

Forever, while the light died in his eyes and they became dark, bottomless, unreadable.

She felt an answering hollowness in her own breast. To have shared such perfect intimacy, to have been gazed at with such devotion and then to have it snatched away...

Oh, good grief. What was she thinking?

'Mr Ravenscar?' She heard the shake in her own voice, but what did her petty feelings matter compared to what he must be going through? 'Dominic, are you all right?' She was too concerned about him to worry about her own feelings and it really was far too late to bother about the formalities of introduction.

'Who are you?' The urgency of her query had apparently got through to him, and when she didn't immediately answer, 'Who the hell are you?' he angrily repeated, rising to his feet, stepping back and putting a yard of distance between them. It felt like a mile. A cold, unbreachable distance. 'What are you doing here?'

Well, what did she expect? *"Thanks for the kiss, ma'am. It was a real pleasure..."*

'I'm Kay Lovell.'

She forced herself to her feet, forced herself to act normally, as if nothing awkward or embarrassing had happened. The kiss had been neither. It was the aftermath that was difficult. Reality, as she'd long ago discovered, was always a lot harder to deal with than fantasy.

She forced herself to brace her knees so that her shaking legs wouldn't collapse beneath her. Maybe kissing was like drinking, she thought. If you didn't do it for a while the effects were amplified…

On the point of offering her hand, she managed to stop herself. It was a little late to be shaking hands. Instead she tried to concentrate on an explanation of what she was doing in his garden. 'I'm just…' No. It was no good. Any attempt to explain what she was doing, explain *anything*, was, for the moment, totally beyond her. And he didn't want to know what she was doing. He just wanted to know why she wasn't his wife. There was no explanation that would satisfy him. No answer that would help. 'I'm just a neighbour,' she said.

He took another step back as if, with every moment that passed, the enormity of his mistake increased. Then he looked beyond her to the peach trees, the newly cut brambles.

'It was you, wasn't it?' he said. 'Yesterday?'

He'd been here then? He'd seen her? She saw all hope die in his eyes and knew he had. Knew what he'd thought. 'Yes, I was here,' she said, guilt washing over her at the damage she'd done. At the forlorn hopes she'd unwittingly raised and then dashed.

'And the child? The little girl?'

She frowned. If he'd seen Polly then surely he must have realised that she couldn't be Sara?

'Who is she?' he persisted.

'My daughter. Polly. We were picking blackberries to make pies for the harvest supper. She's gone out with friends today. To the sea. The Hallams? I think you know them. Their youngest boy is just a few months older and they're best...' She stopped. She was talking far too much. 'I'm so sorry—'

'It doesn't matter,' he snapped, cutting off her apology.

'If I'd known you were home I'd have—'

'You'd have knocked and asked permission?' he enquired, with cutting sarcasm. 'Why did you come back? To make sure you hadn't missed any? Or was there something else you'd taken a fancy to?'

He glanced at the shrub, then at her, raised one brow about half a millimetre—more than enough to imply everything that he was thinking—and she felt the blood rush to her face.

'No! I was just...' She let it go. If he really thought she'd come to steal a shrub that size armed with nothing more than a pocket knife and a screwdriver, there wasn't a thing she could say that would convince him otherwise. 'The lock on the gate was rusted through. I came back to fit a new one. It should hold now. And I—'

'Will it keep you out?' His voice was no longer soft, but hard and cold as ice, perfectly matching the chilling lack of emotion, lack of anything, in his eyes.

'It will if you bolt it behind me,' she managed, with measured politeness, despite the fact that her heart was still pounding like a jackhammer. 'In fact you'd be doing me a favour. I thought I'd have to bolt it from the inside and then climb over and it's rather a long drop.' She made a stab at a smile. He didn't respond. Well, fine. She was in the wrong here, she reminded herself. He had every right to be angry. She gestured vaguely towards the wheelbarrow filled with the thorny trimmings that were destined for her bonfire. 'I'd better go. I've done everything I came for.'

He glanced across at her barrow as if to reassure himself that she wasn't making off with a haul of valuable plants. Frowned when he saw the contents.

'Why did you do that?'

'Fix the gate?'

'Cut back the brambles. Why did you do that?'

'They were growing over the peach tree. It was suffering…' Then, because he didn't say anything, it occurred to her that she'd never have a better chance to put her case for some work. The very worst he could do was throw her out and he was pretty much doing that anyway. 'I'm a gardener. I was going to contact the house agents tomorrow to see if they were interested in giving me some work. To tidy up in here. Now it's on the market.'

'Don't bother,' he said abruptly. 'I like it just the way it is.'

Suffocating. Like him, from the heart outwards.

'You're probably right,' she said, bending down to pick up her hat. 'Better let the new owners clear it out. Start again.'

'Maybe they'll employ you.'

'I doubt that. It'll take months to put this straight. I expect they'll get in a contractor. Someone who can provide instant results with an earthmover. They'll just dump all this in a skip and bring in fully grown plants like they do in those television makeover programmes.'

If she'd hoped to drive the chill from his eyes with hot anger, wake him from the coma of grief, she realised immediately that she was reaching a long way beyond her grasp. He was far beyond such pathetic pseudo-psychological tricks.

All she got was a blank expression.

Of course, he'd been working abroad for a long time. He'd probably never seen one of those programmes where a garden was transformed from backyard tip to easy-care Mediterranean landscape—with water feature—in a weekend. For a man who'd been working on aid programmes, the very idea of such a frivolous waste of resources would probably be anathema.

'Well, I'll go, then. If you need anything, I live at Old Cottage,' she said. 'Just down the lane.'

'What could I possibly need?' Between them hung the unspoken corollary "…from you?"

Nothing was clearly the answer. He was wrong. She could offer human contact. Be there for him, as Amy had been there when she had been lost in depths of despair, guilt. Day after day. Week after week. Gently persistent. Unwavering in the face of rejection. Refusing to be pushed away.

'One day someone will need you, Kay,' she'd said when she'd bemoaned her inability to repay such patient, unasked-for, unrewarded care. 'Just pass on the love and don't count the cost. That's all any of us can do.'

She had a sudden, terrible premonition that this was her moment. And she wasn't ready. Hadn't a clue what to do.

'I could offer you a cup of tea,' she prompted. Oh,

good grief. How English. How predictable. 'Breakfast?' she persisted. 'The eggs are organic. I keep a few hens...'

He didn't reply. Not by one twitch of his facial muscles did he indicate that he'd heard.

For heaven's sake, politeness cost nothing.

'How about a towel to dry your feet?' she tried, but a little waspishly, rapidly losing any desire to pass on anything, let alone care.

He glanced down and frowned as if only then aware that he was wading through damp grass in his bare feet. That his trousers were soaked through to the knees. Then he turned, without a word, and walked back towards the house.

Kay watched him walk away from her. Stiff-backed, rigid with anger and pride and misery. Probably hating himself for having mistaken another woman for his beloved Sara. Hating himself for having kissed another woman.

Yes, well. She knew her limitations. She wasn't wise enough, clever enough for this. Amy should be here. She'd know what to do. Exactly the right words to say.

The one thing she wouldn't do was walk away and leave him like this.

But Amy wasn't here. She was on her way to the coast with Jake and a car-load of children, so it was down to her and, while common sense suggested that it would be wiser to do as he'd asked and leave, simple humanity demanded a braver, a more compassionate response.

'Oh...chickweed!' she muttered. And followed him.

She paused on the threshold of the drawing room. Despite the delicate floral wallpaper, the pale blue curtains, the atmosphere was oppressive, musty.

garden, it felt abandoned. Out there she itched to tear out the weeds, let in the light so the plants could grow, reach their full potential. Inside, she yearned to rush through the rooms, opening the windows to let in the sun, let in the air so that the house could take a deep breath.

She restrained herself. She'd already done enough damage.

There was no sign of Dominic Ravenscar other than an armchair from which the dust sheet had been pulled and left on the floor where it had fallen, suggesting that he'd slept there in front of the open French window. Hoping for another glimpse of his 'Sara'.

That, and wet footprints in the dust leaving a trail across the wide oak floorboards. Guilt more than any mission to do good drove her to follow them across the drawing room and into the hall to where they became dusty marks against the stair carpet.

From the floor above came the sound of running water as he took a shower. She found she'd been holding her breath, anticipating disaster, but that at least had the ring of normality about it. She found the kitchen, washed the green plant stains from her hands under the running tap, then filled the kettle and switched it on.

There was a small box of groceries standing on the table containing tea bags, a small loaf, from which a couple of slices had already been taken, and a carton of long-life milk. She put some bread into the toaster and th⋯ ⋯ted through the cupboards until she found a ⋯ a mug.

⋯g was covered in a film of dust and, while ⋯ water into the bowl, she looked for some ⋯uid. There was a bottle, half empty, in a cupboard beneath the draining board. The manufacturer had changed the packaging several years ago and she had the unsettling feeling that Sara Ravenscar had been the last person to touch it.

Pushing aside the thought as ridiculously melodramatic, she swooshed some into the water and began to rinse the dishes.

What had he done? What on earth had he been thinking? Imagining that Sara was waiting for him in the garden. Talking to her. That woman must have thought he was mad when he'd kissed her.

Maybe he was.

Except it was clear that she'd known who he was, had known exactly what he'd been thinking. Was that why she'd let him embrace her? Hadn't yelled blue murder when he'd kissed her?

Not only had she not struggled, screamed, slapped him, but she'd kissed him back, and for a moment, just a moment, he'd believed that he'd woken up from an endless nightmare. With the soft warmth of a woman's mouth against his, hot life had raced through his veins and he'd felt like a man again.

'Fool!' He smashed his fist against the tiled wall. 'Idiot!' Would he never learn?

There was no hope, only despair that he'd mistaken a stranger for the woman he'd loved. Still loved. Beyond the superficial similarity of colouring, height, they were nothing alike. He'd allowed his mind to trick him. This woman, Kay Lovell,—'Kay Lovell'—he said the name out loud to reinforce the message—was, if anything a little taller, nowhere near as thin. Her eyes were grey rather than blue. Her hair hadn't had the heavy swing, the bright polish...

And she'd let him kiss her out of pity.

He grabbed for the soap, used it to wash his hair, rid himself of the fresh-air smell of her. Brushed his teeth to rid himself of the taste of her mouth on his.

There was no simple remedy for the pounding in his veins. The shocking response of his body to a total stranger.

That was a betrayal he was going to have to live with.

And he grabbed a towel, wrapped it about his waist. Then, since he'd only brought up his overnight bag, he went downstairs to fetch the rest of his luggage.

Kay made tea in the mug, then began buttering the toast. When she looked up, Dominic Ravenscar was standing in the doorway, watching her, his expression blank, unreadable. As if he'd had years of practising keeping his thoughts, his feelings, to himself.

He'd showered. His dark hair was damp and tousled where he hadn't bothered to comb it—well, he hadn't been expecting company—and he was naked but for a towel wrapped about his waist. There was little of him she couldn't see and it was plain that this was a man who'd lost every bit of softness from his body as well as his heart.

'You're still here.'

'There's nothing wrong with your eyesight,' she agreed. As the words left her lips she groaned inwardly. Even twenty-twenty vision could be fooled by the heart.

'Did Greg send you?' he demanded.

'Greg?' She sucked the butter from her thumb, a distraction from the spare, sinewy shoulders, ribs that she'd be able to count with her fingers if she walked them down his chest. There was not an ounce of spare flesh on him.

'Did he ask you to keep an eye on me?'

'No one sent me.'

'You're just an all-round busybody and do-gooder, is that it?'

What did she expect? Gratitude?

Had she been grateful when Amy had found her, taken her home, found ways to get her to eat—even if it was only chocolate; ways to get Polly into her arms and her to start living again?

No.

She'd just wanted to be left alone. She'd just wanted to die. She thought perhaps they had more in common than he'd ever know. He just wanted her to go, forget he'd ever set eyes on her, forget that he'd kissed her. No doubt he thought that being rude was not only the quickest way to get rid of her, but the most likely way to ensure that she'd stay out of his hair.

She'd tried that approach, too. In fact his response brought her own hateful ingratitude shamefully to mind. She'd been rude, too. Vilely rude. It hadn't worked. Amy had seen through the anger to the pain and stuck with it.

She dunked the tea bag, added milk to the mug and offered it to him. 'You haven't got any sugar, so I assume you don't take it. You haven't got any marmalade for the toast, either.'

'I haven't got much of anything except you,' he said, ignoring the mug. 'You, I have altogether too much of.'

'That's how it is with us do-gooders,' she said, putting the tea down on the table where he could reach it. 'I'll bring you a pot of mine. It's very good. It won best-in-show at the summer fête.'

'Congratulations, but don't put yourself out. I don't like marmalade.'

'Strawberry jam?' she offered. It was as if her mouth had a mind of its own. 'I used organic, home-grown strawberries. It won best in its class.' She snapped her mouth shut.

'What do you want?' he persisted.

'Nothing,' she said. 'Absolutely nothing.'

'Good, because that's what you've got.' And he picked up the tea and tipped it down the sink.

She swallowed, stunned at how much that had hurt. But then it was meant to. She knew all the moves.

'You prefer coffee?' She didn't make the mistake of offering to make him some, but said, 'I'll remember that for next time. In the meantime, if you need anything you know where to find me.' And without waiting for him to respond, to tell her to get lost, stay away, she walked back out into the garden.

Back to the witch hazel she'd been rescuing when he'd kissed her.

Her head told her to keep going, but she refused to leave a job half done and she knelt down to finish her rescue mission. Only when she attempted to unravel the tightly coiled stem of the bindweed did she discover that her hands were shaking so much that she was forced to tuck them beneath her arms to hold them still.

Dom picked up the toast and, tight-lipped, he tossed it in the bin. Then he picked up his bags and carried them upstairs to the bedroom he'd shared for one sweet, perfect year with Sara.

Last night the only scent he'd been aware of was the lingering ghost of her perfume clinging to her clothes.

He dropped his suitcase and strained to find it again, to cling to that last lingering essence of the woman he loved.

But it evaded him. Today, the only smell was that of a house locked up and unlived-in for too long. And he opened a window.

CHAPTER THREE

"Long live the weeds and the wilderness yet."
                              Gerard Manley Hopkins

DOM LINGERED at the window to breathe in the fresh, green scent of the garden, of newly turned earth, and looked beyond the walls to where the picture-perfect village was laid out before him.

Nothing had changed.

Not the carefully mown section of the village green where cricket was played every weekend in the summer before the teams retired to the pub to continue their rivalries on the dart board. Not the rougher grassland of the common, where willows dipped over the stream-fed pond that teemed with tadpoles in the spring, moorhens nested and a donkey was, even now, cropping grass on the end of a long tether.

It could even be the same donkey.

It was exactly the right place to bring up a family, Sara had said, utterly charmed from the moment they'd set eyes on the place. It was so safe.

But nothing was that perfect and every Eden had its serpent. Hidden, insidious dangers. He looked down into the wreck of the garden. It had taken everything from him. To look at its beauty had been an agony and he'd run from it. But Sara had loved it and to see it like this, neglected, overgrown, was somehow worse.

A movement on the green caught his attention and he

looked away, grateful for the distraction. At least he was until he realised that it was Kay Lovell heading for the village-shop-cum-post-office-cum-everything, to fetch a pint of milk, or the Sunday newspaper.

The warmth of her smile reached his window as she stopped to speak to someone, exchange the time of day. No prizes for guessing the subject of their conversation. The news that the house was on the market would be the hot subject of gossip this morning. By tomorrow, he had no doubt, everyone in the village would know that he was back, courtesy of his blackberry-raiding neighbour. Back home and losing his mind.

He watched her continue on her errand, long-limbed and lithe, striding across the green, and wondered again how he could ever have mistaken her for Sara. They were not in the least bit alike.

It had been just a trick of the imagination, tiredness perhaps, that had fooled him. Or maybe just that she was there, in Sara's place, doing the things that she would have been doing...

He wrenched his gaze away from her and looked back at the garden. From above, he could clearly see the peach tree freed from its bramble prison, the fresh, clear patch of earth around the shrub where she'd been weeding, and, furious with himself—with her—he clattered down the stairs, raced down the garden, sliding the bolt into place on the gate before turning and leaning with his back to it, eyes closed, while he regained his breath. He didn't want her, or any more sightseers, invading the privacy of the garden. It wasn't fit to be seen. And with a roar of anguish he grabbed the agent's For Sale sign and wrenched the post out of the ground.

* * *

Kay dropped her newspaper on the dresser. With a rare morning to herself, she'd planned a lazy hour with her feet up with the colour supplement and the gardening pages, but now she was home she was all of a twitch and there was no way she could sit still.

Never mind. She'd work off her nervous energy doing something practical. She had pastry to make, harvest pies to fill and freeze, and there was no time like the present.

Forget Dominic Ravenscar, she told herself as she washed her hands and got out the scales. Forget the way he'd kissed her. It wasn't *her* he'd been kissing, she reminded herself as she shovelled flour from the bin onto the scales with hands that weren't altogether steady.

He'd thought she was his wife. A *ghost*, for pity's sake.

And she'd been tempted to play amateur psychologist? She should be grateful that he'd made it absolutely clear that he never wanted to set eyes on her again.

She took a deep, steadying breath, then dumped another scoop into the scales.

What the devil did she think she could do in ten minutes with a cup of tea and a slice of toast, anyway? She wasn't Amy Hallam with her gift for seeing through to the heart of the matter. For making *you* see it too.

She stared blankly at the pile of flour and tried to recall what she was doing.

Pastry.

She was making pastry.

Right.

'He couldn't have made it plainer that he didn't want me anywhere near him or his garden,' she said. Asleep on top of the boiler, Mog wasn't taking any notice, but talking to the cat had to be better than talking to herself. Marginally.

'He didn't actually tell me what I could do with my "tea and sympathy",' she continued, despite the lack of feline encouragement. 'Not in so many words. But then why would he bother, when his actions spoke for him? Loud and clear.'

The cat opened one eye, sighed and closed it again.

'OK, so you had to be there.'

And what exactly was she complaining about, anyway? So he'd poured away the tea she'd made him. That was rude by anyone's standards, but, to be fair, he hadn't asked her to make it. Hadn't asked for her concern, either. She'd foisted herself on him and he'd made no bones about unfoisting her in double-quick time.

She should be relieved. She'd got momentarily carried away with noble aspirations that were not in the least bit appreciated. She was the one who was out of line. Luckily, he had made it easy to walk away with a clear conscience.

'I should be relieved,' she said. She *was* relieved.

'It isn't as if I don't have anything better to do.' She fetched the butter and lard from the fridge and began to chop it up into small pieces with rather more vigour than was actually called for. 'I'm a single mother with a child to raise. A cat to support. I don't need any more complications in my life.'

Chop, chop, chop.

Not that Polly was anything other than a joy. But still. Parenthood, even with a complete set of parents, required absolute concentration. Alone it was...

Chop, chop. The snap of the heavy blade against the board happily cut short this train of thought.

One kiss and suddenly she felt lonely? When did she have time to get lonely?

'I'm a single mother with a child to raise and a business that's going nowhere,' she informed the cat briskly.

Chop.

The cat yawned.

'And let's not forget the part-time job in the village shop. That's more than enough work for one woman. I don't need Dominic Ravenscar and his problems complicating my life any further.'

Chop, chop, chop, chop.

'As for his garden—'

But Mog, realising that she wasn't going to get any more peace, stood up, stretched, then jumped down and walked out of the kitchen, her tail aquiver with disgust.

'Oh, great. The least you could do is lend a sympathetic ear in return for all the meaty chunks you stuff down. No more top-of-the-milk treats for you, you ungrateful creature.'

All she got in reply was a disdainful flick of the tail as Mog headed towards a patch of catnip growing near the path.

'And I'll dig that up, too,' she warned.

The cat, recognising an empty threat when she heard it, nuzzled the plant, a blissful expression on her face.

'I'll dig it up and plant something useful. Onions. Garlic, even,' she threatened. 'Then you'll be sorry.'

Which was another thing. Any time and energy she had to spare were needed for her own garden. You couldn't make prize-winning strawberry jam unless you put in the time at the strawberry beds.

And even if she wanted the chance to clear up the Linden Lodge garden—OK, she *did* want it, rather des-

perately—she didn't have time to take on the role of
Dominic Ravenscar's personal agony aunt. Always supposing he wanted her to. Which he plainly didn't.

That *was* time-consuming. Amy had spent *hours* just
being there for her. Days. Weeks. Even now all she had
to do was pick up the telephone…

Not that she had to. Polly's godmother usually found
an excuse to drop in most days. Sometimes, it felt as if
she was being checked up on… She backed away from
that ungrateful thought even as it surfaced, dealing with
the remainder of the shortening in double-quick time.

It wasn't just that she was busy. She was a single
mother living in a gossipy village and, having worked
hard to gain the respect of the community, she was going
to take good care to keep it.

A broken-hearted widower popping in day and night
for tea and sympathy—no matter how innocent his
needs, how noble her motives—would soon set the
tongues wagging in the post-office queue.

Which was quite enough of Dominic Ravenscar.

She picked up the sieve and realised she hadn't got
out the mixing bowl.

Normally the most organised person on earth, she was
all at sixes and sevens, her hard-won calm shattered by
a kiss that had, for a moment, brought every long-
suppressed womanly feeling bubbling to the surface.

She took another deep breath. 'Forget it,' she said. To
herself this time, since the cat's listening skills were
clearly limited to the sound of a tin being opened. But
then, that was how it was. Just her and Polly. And she
wasn't about to burden her daughter with her loneliness.
Or disturb the even tenor of their lives by getting involved with a man. 'Forget him.'

Easier said than done, and she only just managed to field the heavy bowl as it slipped through her buttery fingers.

Dominic wanted to roar his anger, his pain, to the heavens, but what would be the point? Who would be listening?

Instead, he flung down the For Sale board and walked back to where Kay Lovell had been working. She must have stayed to finish the job, he realised, looking at the delicate shrub, freed from its prison of bindweed, standing in its own clear patch of earth.

Definitely not listening.

But although her barrow and tools were gone, she'd left something behind. By accident or intention?

He bent to pick up her pocket knife from where it had fallen in the crushed grass, immediately quashing the suspicion. Why on earth would she want an excuse to return?

He'd been ill-mannered—

No, that was too kind.

He'd been damned rude—not unusual; it was a well-rehearsed method for ridding himself of anyone who attempted to get close—when it didn't take half a brain to see that an apology would have been wiser. More than damned rude. He'd as good as accused her of stealing valuable plants when what she'd actually been doing was rescuing one of Sara's precious shrubs from the stranglehold of neglect.

Slander was the least of it, though. Considering he'd just kissed her with an intimacy that had left him shaking to his soul, he was probably fortunate that he wasn't looking at a charge of assault. The small matter of her trespass wouldn't save him.

The truth of the matter was that he'd made a total fool of himself, yet she hadn't reacted with horror, hadn't betrayed the slightest sign of embarrassment or annoyance, even when he'd shouted at her as if it had somehow been her fault that she wasn't Sara. Instead she'd shown concern, made him tea and toast, offered him a jar of her home-made marmalade, for heaven's sake. Exactly the kind of thoughtful, caring neighbour they'd anticipated finding in the perfect English village.

The kind of person who helped themselves to blackberries growing wild in your garden, but then did a little gardening to leave it looking better than she'd found it. As if she were fifty, rather than somewhere in her mid-twenties.

Of course, if she'd been a middle-aged do-gooder he wouldn't have kissed her. Nor would she have responded with such melting warmth. That had been rather more than neighbourly. As was the vital, urgent way his body had reacted to the taste of her mouth, the softness of her lips as they'd parted beneath the onslaught of his need, his yearning to take her, there in the long, soft grass.

He could almost believe that she would have been a willing surrogate, surrendering to his clamouring need. And his body, so long dormant, only half alive, quickened at the thought.

Kay set the bowl carefully on the table, washed her hands and, after a couple of deep breaths, continued with the task she'd set herself, refusing to succumb to a fit of girlish trembles over a kiss.

Double-checking the weight. Putting a jug of water in

the fridge to chill. Shaking out her fingers to relax them. If she was knotted up with tension the pastry would be like lead. She'd already forgotten the salt. As she reached for it, her elbow caught the edge of the scales. It would have been wiser to let it fall; that way the mess would have been confined to the table.

Her wild grab to save it made things ten times worse as it flew into the air and the flour exploded in a white, choking cloud.

'Oh…dandelions!' she yelled, flapping her hand around in an attempt to clear the air, but only making things worse, and she stumbled outside into the garden, coughing and spluttering, her eyes watering.

She wiped them on her apron. Blinked. Then forgot to breathe at all as she saw Dominic Ravenscar standing at her gate. Tall, dark and, from the way her heart rate accelerated, extremely dangerous to her peace of mind, despite the fact that he was now safely clad in a pair of faded jeans and a polo shirt.

As if she hadn't already discovered the danger. Why else was she trembling?

For a moment neither of them spoke.

'I wanted to—'

'I had a bit of—'

They both stopped.

Kay swallowed, said, 'I had a bit of an accident with some flour.'

'I would never have guessed.'

He wasn't just plain rude, then. He did sarcasm, too. Great.

'Clown face, huh?' she said, lifting her forearm to her cheek in an attempt to brush the worst of the flour away, but probably only making things worse. 'Is this a social call or did you change your mind about the strawberry jam?' she asked, rather more sharply than she'd intended.

So much for her empathy skills.

'No, thank you. I do, however, owe you an apology.'

Kay bit back the urge to fill the silence with an assurance that it was OK. Forget it. He'd had a shock and she understood.

He'd been rude. Damn rude. So she held her peace and waited.

'And I thought you might be looking for this,' he said, taking her gardening knife from his pocket and holding it up so that she could see it.

She felt her cheeks flame up—just to complete the clown image—as she hoped against hope that it wasn't *her* precious knife but another one, exactly like it. And how likely was that? But she slapped at the pocket in her cargo trousers where she always kept it, anyway. One thing had to go right today.

It was empty.

Of course.

As a mother she'd learned to curb the language she'd learned in the terrible months when she was alone, replacing the forbidden words with the names of the more irritatingly pernicious weeds in times of extreme provocation or stress. There were plenty of them to choose from. But for once she was left speechless.

Dropping her precious knife looked so much like some deliberate ploy, an excuse to pay a return visit. He could take his pick of reasons for that.

Frustrated single mother looking for an advance on his early-morning kiss.

Meddling busybody eager to get stuck into someone else's problems.

Desperate jobbing gardener hoping for work.

He'd certainly never believe it was unintentional. In his shoes, she wouldn't believe it either.

"Chickweed" didn't cover this one. Neither did "dandelions". This was a fully blown "ground elder" moment because of the three she suspected that he was most likely to believe that she was some desperate female looking for a repeat performance of this morning. In view of her enthusiastic response.

She only hoped that he wasn't right. That subconsciously she hadn't—

'May I?' he enquired, rescuing her from the nightmare scenario of her own thoughts, as he indicated the gate. He didn't wait for an invitation, but opened it, walked up the path towards her and came to a halt a few feet away.

'I'm sorry,' he said.

'What for?' Oh, dumb question!

'This morning.'

Her hot cheeks, which had begun to cool, flamed again.

'I shouldn't have suggested you were stealing plants,' he said.

Oh. Right. That *was* bad. She cleared her throat. Then, before she could manage an answer, she had to clear it again. 'I can understand why you'd be suspicious. Not too many people break into gardens to do the weeding.'

For a moment he stared at her, then he said, 'No, I don't suppose they do.'

Well, that fell flat. He was supposed to laugh. At least smile. Considering she'd been so gracious.

'I apologise for tipping away the tea, too. It was...'

Since being gracious hadn't made much of an impression and he appeared to be at something of a loss for an appropriate word, she supplied the one she thought fitted the situation best. 'Petty?'

His mouth tightened.

'Just a bit childish?' she offered, since he didn't appear to appreciate her first suggestion.

'Ungrateful,' he said. And he moved his shoulders in what might, just, have been a shrug. 'I suppose I should go the whole hog and confess that I threw away the toast, too.'

'Well, now I'm shocked,' she declared. Just as it occurred to her that maybe he was the one who'd needed an excuse to call. That maybe her unaccountable carelessness *had* been the result of her subconscious working overtime when she wasn't looking. Maybe it knew more than she did.

Maybe she was fooling herself.

'You do know there are starving people out there?' she said. His face remained expressionless, his eyes giving nothing away, and she realised that he had no way of knowing when she was teasing, when she was being serious. 'Of course you do. That's what you do, isn't it? Aid work?' When he didn't reply, she relented. 'OK, I'll forgive you this once. Only because you didn't ask me to make it and I guess busybody do-gooders must expect the occasional knock back.'

He shook his head, and this time when his mouth tightened it edged nearer to a smile. Possibly. Which was something of a relief.

'Perhaps I should make a donation to the vicar's fund for famine relief,' he offered. 'Would that put it right?'

'Oh, look, I didn't mean… You've done your bit. You don't…' She stopped herself, suddenly realising that she was being teased back. 'I'm sure he'd appreciate that.'

'Consider it done.' The almost-smile died. 'Actually, what I really wanted to say—'

'No. Stop right there.' No woman wanted to hear a man say he was sorry for kissing her. 'That's quite enough apologising. This morning is wiped from the slate.' She held out her hand, accepted the pocket knife. It was still warm from his hand, his body. 'Thanks for returning this. I don't know what I would have done without it.'

'Broken in through the gate again?' he offered.

'Oh, that's a low blow. I'll have you know that when I fix a bolt, Mr Ravenscar, it stays fixed.'

'I guess you'd have had to climb over the wall, then. When you were quite sure I was not at home—'

She was grateful for that.

'—and rescued another shrub from certain death while you were there, no doubt.'

'I always find it hard to resist temptation.' Which was probably not the brightest response in the world. But she still found herself close to smiling as she turned and walked back into her kitchen, leaving him to follow or not, as he chose. When she turned he was standing in the opening, blocking out the sunlight so that his face was in shadow.

'About the garden,' he said.

Her heart gave a little flutter that wasn't entirely connected with the possibility of some work. 'Yes?'

'You're right. It is in a terrible state. I'd like to have it restored, put back the way it was before…'

He couldn't say the words, she realised. 'Before it wasn't in a terrible state?' she offered.

He glanced out at her own garden, crammed to over-flowing with cottage favourites. 'You seem to know what you're doing.'

Kay reached for the kettle, clamping her mouth firmly shut to prevent herself from telling him that she was more than interested. Gripping it tightly while she filled it in order to prevent herself from flinging her arms around him and demonstrating exactly how interested she was.

Throwing her arms around him would not be a good idea. And certainly not professional. Tempting, but not wise.

Like taking the job, she realised with a sinking heart.

It would be a great business opportunity for her, of course it would. A terrific selling point for her embryo company that she had begun with such high hopes. By now she'd imagined it would have taken off sufficiently for her to buy a decent van, take on some help, but it was still bumping along at ground level.

Oh, right. As if she cared about any of that. She wanted to do it for the pure pleasure, the personal sat-isfaction of working in the peace and calm of the walled garden. Restoring something beautiful, bringing it back to life.

But much as she wanted to grab it with both hands, she needed to forget her own needs here and concentrate on Dominic Ravenscar. The one thing she had learned this morning was that he had not come to terms with his loss, and she was almost certain that seeing her at work in the garden his wife had made would not do anything to help him let go.

In fact she was almost certain he was choosing her more for the similarity in their appearance than for her gardening skills. To feed his fantasy that she was still somehow...*there*.

She might not be any great shakes when it came to psychology, but she had a very strong feeling that restoring the garden would not be in Dominic Ravenscar's best interests. At least not this way.

'To be honest, I was just looking for a few hours' work clearing the place up,' she said. 'Making it look tidy so that it wouldn't put off potential buyers. I've done that before. Estate agents use me for that and for the gardens of their rental properties because I'm cheap.' If he thought that she was a complete no-hoper with ideas way above her skills, so be it. 'Total restoration is something else. It's a major project and you're going to need a proper landscape-gardening company for that. Someone with plenty of staff. They'll give you a quote for the whole job so that you'll know how much it will cost up front.' All this was true, but she still had to swallow hard as she threw away such an opportunity. 'It would probably work out less expensive to do it that way,' she added. 'In the long run. I'd take forever.'

'Despite the fact that you're cheap?'

'I'm only just starting out,' she said. 'I have to give companies a good reason to employ me. Once I'm known as reliable, I'll be able to charge a more realistic rate.' The truth was that when she'd costed the full price of her labour, with overheads, transport and allowing for the possibility of taking on someone young and fit to do some of the heavy work, she'd quite lost her nerve.

'Once you're known as cheap, no one will ever pay you a realistic rate,' he responded. 'The word will go round and you'll be forced to accept the minimum, while your friendly estate agents will no doubt pass on the charge to their clients at the maximum the market will bear. You need to value yourself if you want other people to take you seriously.'

'What makes you different?'

'Cost is not a factor in this case. Nor is time. What I need is someone who cares about the garden.'

She ignored this call to her wallet. 'Who says I care?'

It was his turn to let silence do the talking for him. Which would teach her to go all bleeding-heart over a peach tree in trouble. Doing CPR on a witch hazel that was being slowly strangled by bindweed.

'You're going to sell the house, Mr Ravenscar,' she said, her voice firm enough, but the rest of her very wobbly indeed. His motives might be mixed, but so were hers. She wasn't at all certain whether she was being frank with him, totally honest, or just running scared. Of the job. Of the responsibility. Of the man. 'Just let it go.'

The advice, at least, was sincerely meant.

'I promise you there won't be a repeat of what happened this morning,' he said stiffly. 'If that's what's bothering you.'

'No!' she declared. Then, confronted by his mouth, her memory inconveniently supplied a vivid recollection of their first encounter and she coloured up again. This morning was still very fresh in her mind and she suspected his, too, or he wouldn't have brought it up. Not that she doubted his assurance for one moment. It was Sara he'd wanted. In his head it had been her he'd been kissing.

Even so, if he was set on this, he'd be better off with

some beefy bloke who wouldn't wrench at his heart-strings whenever he caught sight of him bent over the perennial border.

'Forget this morning. I have,' she said, her flushed cheeks betraying her, even as she crossed her fingers behind her back. She would never forget the magic of that kiss. 'It'll take me months to get your garden back to the way it was and I've already got a part-time job at the village shop as well as my regular clients.'

'I see.' His jaw tightened. 'Are you telling me that you won't do it?'

'I'm saying that maybe I'm not the best person for the job.'

'That's an unusual way of building a business.'

'Maybe. But I'm being honest here. I really think you need to think about it.'

'I have thought about it. Sara spent so much time and effort designing, planting, tending...' His voice died away and for a moment he seemed to be somewhere else. Then, realising that she was looking at him, 'I don't want it destroyed. If it's in good order, looking as she left it, there won't be the temptation for the buyers to rip it all out and start again.'

Damn. She was sure he hadn't been taking any real notice when she'd been playing Freud. His response to her reality check was apparently to turn the place into a lasting memorial to his wife.

Was that a good thing? Or was it just asking for trouble? And was it really any of her business?

CHAPTER FOUR

"With burdocks, hemlock, nettles, cuckoo-flowers,
Darnel, and all the idle weeds that grow..."
William Shakespeare

'I CAN'T...I won't let anyone see it the way it is,' he said abruptly, as if he knew exactly what she was thinking.

'You'll have a job to sell the house if you won't let anyone see the garden,' she pointed out.

'I'm going to call the agent tomorrow and take it off the market until the garden is fixed. How long that will take is down to you.'

'Oh, now, wait. You can't—'

'How many hours a week can you spare?'

He wasn't going to take no for an answer, she realised, but despite the little lift in her own heart she was determined to give it one last go. Try and make him see how impossible it was.

'Ten hours, maximum. My mornings are pretty much taken up so I can only give you my afternoons. Two hours, five afternoons a week.'

'Two?' he repeated. 'Two hours? That's an afternoon's work? You don't push yourself, do you?'

'For a man who seems desperate to employ me, you aren't going out of your way to be polite,' she responded, losing her practised calm in the face of his rudeness. 'For your information I finish at three-fifteen when Polly comes home from school.' It was one of the

reasons she chose to work for herself. 'That is not ne-
gotiable.'

As the kettle began to whistle on the Aga, she turned
away to move it from the heat and had to force herself
not to take another deep breath—at this rate she'd be
hyperventilating. And her pulse could behave itself and
stop fluttering right now. It was time to put a stop to
this.

'That's the best I can offer, Mr Ravenscar,' she said
formally. 'Thank you for thinking of me, giving me the
opportunity to undertake what will, I'm sure, be a very
rewarding job. But, as I've already told you, you're going to need full-time help if you want this done in the
foreseeable future.'

'I know what I need, Ms Lovell,' he replied, immediately picking up her tone and responding with equal
formality. 'I need you. If two hours each weekday afternoon is all you can give me, then so be it. Until further
notice. At a realistic hourly rate. Can we shake hands
on that?'

There was the gleam of something that might have
been a challenge behind a pair of very dark eyes. As if
he knew she was running scared.

On the point of showing him who was scared, she
lifted her hand in automatic response. It was still covered
with flour.

'I think you should sleep on it,' she said, rubbing her
hands down her apron in a belated move to avoid the
one he'd extended. Suggesting that it was her floury
hand she was saving him from rather than a binding
commitment. She needed time to think about it. Come
up with some really convincing reason why he shouldn't
be doing this. Why she shouldn't be going along with

him. 'And in the meantime I'll check and see what other work I have in my diary for the next couple of months.'

'There can't be much if you have to work in the village shop to make ends meet,' he pointed out.

'You see?' she declared. 'There you go again. Being downright rude. I guess you just can't help yourself. I'll have you know I *enjoy* working in the village shop.'

'Really? How much? Do you, for instance, break in there and stack shelves out of hours?'

'I did not "break in"'—she used her floury fingers to make quotation marks—'to your garden! I pushed the gate and it opened. The bolt loop had rusted through. I did you a favour!'

'Fine. You can add the cost of fitting the new bolt to your first month's invoice.'

'In the meantime,' she said, pointedly ignoring this further provocation—she'd already done more than enough to demonstrate that she was not the kind of woman anyone in their right mind would want to employ—and taking one of the leaflets she'd produced on her aged computer out of the dresser drawer, 'you might like to look at this. It sets out my terms. And my experience.'

'Nil, if this is how you conduct your business.'

She ignored that. 'It'll take a lot of work and, while I may be cheap, I'm not *that* cheap.'

'Are you suggesting that I might not be able to afford you, Ms Lovell?' he asked, taking the leaflet but not looking at it. 'Despite your cut-price rates.'

'Anyone who leaves a valuable property empty to moulder for six years probably has more money than sense,' she responded. Oh, great. That was professional... 'I'm simply suggesting that you shouldn't rush into anything, Mr Ravenscar.' Then, 'I work in the village shop tomorrow morning until one o'clock. I'll call in on my way home and you can let me know if you want to proceed then. You will be at home?'

'Home?' He frowned. 'Oh, I see. It doesn't matter. I'll leave the gate unbolted. Bring your tools with you and you can start work right away.' With that, he nodded, and before she could ask him if he would like that cup of coffee he'd gone.

Actually, that was probably just as well. He'd already demonstrated what he thought of her catering, and if she was going to work in his garden she didn't want any confusion about who she was. It would be much wiser to keep it strictly professional.

Mr Ravenscar and Ms Lovell.

Right.

The man might have forgotten how to live, but he certainly knew how to give orders. Start work right away. Of course, sir. Three bags full, sir. Why would she need to have lunch?

So much for empathy. For her fanciful notion of paying forward the debt that she owed Amy Hallam. Forget "being there" for him. At this rate she was more likely to crown the wretched man with her stainless-steel spade and put him out of his misery permanently.

She cleared up the flour, then began again, this time putting all her concentration into making the pastry before setting it in the fridge to relax. Only then did she make herself the promised coffee and take it outside to sit in the sun and reassure herself that she was doing the right thing in shying away from the Linden Lodge job.

Things weren't that bad. OK, so work was slow to come in but she had a few steady clients in the village.

She took care of Mike and Willow Armstrong's garden,
for instance. It was extremely low maintenance; a gravel
and paved courtyard and a paddock for the children to
run wild in. All she had to do was pluck out the occasional weed and keep the pots filled with seasonal plants.
She suspected they'd taken her on out of charity, just to
encourage her. But it was a job.

The Hilliards, in the Old Rectory, gave her a couple
of hours a week, too, and she regularly mowed the lawn
for some of the pensioners. Of course, they couldn't afford to pay her, but instead knitted little things for Polly.
Her daughter had more woolly hats and mittens than she
would ever be able to wear in one lifetime. Maybe she
should organise them all into a collective, channel their
energies in something saleable and set up a stall in
Maybridge market. Then they could pay her in hard
cash.

No, no… Concentrate.

The hard truth was that two hours' work every afternoon would make a big difference to her finances. A big
difference to Polly, whose sixth birthday was coming up
fast and about to overtake her on the blind side. Polly,
who wanted a party in the village hall. And a bicycle.
And deserved both.

So what if there was something about Dominic
Ravenscar that unsettled her, made her remember all the
things that she was missing, that most young women
took for granted? Romance. Love. Sex…

She was grown up. She could handle it.

It would have been easier without the memory-
jogging early-morning close encounter with his mouth.
But she could handle it.

In the meantime, what she needed was vigorous

exercise to distract her from the memory of Mr Ravenscar's square shoulders, his naked chest, hips that had narrowed appealingly beneath his towel.

Her breasts crushed against that same chest.

Her hips nestled against...

This would, she decided, be a very good moment to turn the compost heap.

'He kissed you? Dominic Ravenscar *kissed* you?'

Polly, having rushed in to say she was back, paused only long enough to exclaim that she'd had '...a brilliant day...' and dump her belongings before rushing out again to race around the green with the Hallam boys after being cooped up in a car for longer than infant flesh and blood could stand. Which left Kay with an opportunity to tell Amy all about her close encounter with her neighbour.

'Not *me*,' she explained. 'It was quite clear that he thought I was a vision, or a ghost, or something. Of his wife.'

'And now he wants you to work for him? You must have been very convincing.'

'Must I?' There was something a little bit ''off'' about Amy's tone, although on reflection, to someone hearing about it cold, it must sound a bit odd, but it was difficult to explain what exactly had happened. 'Maybe he was just relieved that I didn't crack him round the head with a weeding fork,' she said, hoping to raise a smile.

'Maybe he was.' No smile. 'Why didn't you?'

'Good question. I guess you had to be there.' Then, 'It was all over in a moment.' A long moment. One of those moments that seemed to go on forever.

'There are moments. And then again there are moments,' Amy said, with that uncanny knack she had for knowing exactly what she was thinking at any given time. 'He probably doesn't know why he's offering you work.'

It was too late to wish she hadn't said anything. She'd thought that if anyone would understand, Amy would. 'And you do?'

'It doesn't take a genius, Kay.' Then, 'You're not seriously thinking of taking it?'

Actually, she hadn't been. All day she'd been working through the pros and cons. There were a lot of ''pros'' but she had, reluctantly, come down on the side of the ''cons'', basically for the same objections that Amy was raising now. But it was one thing to make a decision for yourself; it was quite another to have someone tell you what you should be doing. Questioning your judgement before they'd even heard you out. Just lately Amy had been doing that a lot. Always there, every time she turned around. Always offering advice as if she knew what was best. For her. For Polly. Especially for Polly.

Good advice, even if it was well meant, had a tendency to become irritating.

'He wouldn't take no for an answer,' she said, refusing to commit herself to an outright yes or no. 'I told him I'd think about it. And that he should do the same.'

'OK, so think about it. And then say no.'

And more than a little patronising.

'That's a bit harsh, Amy.'

'I'm thinking of you, Kay. He's an attractive man, but one who clearly needs help. Grief counselling at the very least.'

'Yes, I can see that for myself.' She had been going to say more, but stopped herself.

'What?'

'Nothing. Forget it.'

'What?' Amy repeated.

She shrugged. 'Do you remember saying to me once—when I tried to thank you for all you'd done for me—that one day I'd see someone who needed me?'

'And you think Dominic Ravenscar is that person?'

'He needs someone.'

There was a thoughtful pause, then Amy said, 'That must have been some kiss.'

She felt her cheeks flush hot. This morning she'd given the whole thing the most careful consideration, thought of her reputation, remembered how hard it had been to get local people to accept her. And she'd made her decision based on reason and common sense.

But she'd had a whole day—without the distraction of a lively little girl to keep her mind from wandering—for that kiss to do its seductive work on her mind, to stir up feelings that she'd buried deep. Now, confronted by Amy's unexpectedly judgemental response, all that yearning need bubbled over into anger. She'd proved herself a good mother, a good friend and a good member of the community. She didn't have to pay for what she'd done for the rest of her life. Did she?

'You don't think I'm up to it, is that it? That I should just keep my head down and stick to mowing lawns for the OAPs—'

Amy put a hand on her arm, stopping her in full flow. 'I'm sorry, Kay. I didn't mean to put you down. You've turned your life around and your compassion does you credit. I'm just surprised that you can't see the danger.'

'Danger?' she demanded. 'What danger?' As if she hadn't been thinking about it all day. If she hadn't seen the danger, she wouldn't have hesitated, she'd have grabbed the job with both hands. 'I'm going to be weeding his borders...' Even as she said the words, she realised she'd been fooling herself with her reasoned arguments. Of course she was going to take the job.

'You're going to make me spell it out for you?'

'I think you'd better.' She heard herself say the words and, horrified, wanted to call them back. This was getting out of hand. OK, her pride was at stake here, but Amy was her friend, her mentor, but now they were on the brink of the kind of argument that could shatter the strongest relationship.

'It's been six years, Kay. You haven't even looked at a man in all that time, but you're young and healthy and suddenly this dark stranger waltzes out of the morning mist and kisses you to within an inch of your life. Putting your hormones in a spin. Reminding you what you've been missing all these years. It would be enough to turn the head of even the most level-headed woman.'

'And I'm not level-headed?'

'I think that right now you're as confused as he is—'

'I'm nearly twenty-five years old, Amy,' she cut in, raising her voice. 'Believe me, I know the difference between fantasy and reality. I've been—'

'—and I would strongly advise staying well clear of a man who'll give you nothing but grief.'

Amy didn't think she knew that? She'd been battling with it all day. Common sense versus a need to stretch herself, prove to herself that she was healed. That she wasn't an emotional cripple who would always need a prop. The fact that she'd been there, too, meant that in reaching out a helping hand she could offer more than compassion.

Someone had to do it.

'He's asked me to fix his garden,' she said, stubbornly. 'That's all.'

'But you think you can fix his heart, too.'

There was no fooling Amy Hallam. 'You fixed mine.'

'I guess the proof of that is the fact that you're prepared to risk it again.' Amy leaned forward, put her arm around Kay and kissed her. 'Thank you for loaning me Polly for the day. It was a joy. But right now I have to go home and soak my aching limbs. I'll have one of the boys bring our little girl home when they've finished letting off steam.'

Polly could barely keep her eyes open in the bath and she was asleep before Kay had picked up the big book of stories and poems that they shared at bedtime.

She tucked her in, kissed her goodnight, but didn't leave her for a long time. Instead she knelt by the bed, watching her, gently stroking the golden down on her cheek, needing to touch her. Reassure herself that she was there. Real.

She'd been so ashamed of what she'd done, so grateful for a second chance, and she was in no doubt that she owed all she had to Amy Hallam. But today, just for a moment, she'd been made to feel like a child herself. Incapable of making her own decisions. And even though she'd stepped back from the brink of an argument with her usual tact and grace, the resentment lingered.

Kay crossed to the window, looked out at the high-walled garden of Linden Lodge. Maybe Amy did know best. Maybe her warning was wise. It was undoubtedly well-meant. But she needed to break free, not spend the rest of her life looking over her shoulder, checking that her mentor approved before she took a step into the unknown.

She couldn't rely on a support structure built on the Hallams' charity for the rest of her life. Living in Amy's cottage. Playing at being a businesswoman as and when it fitted in with the rest of her life. Sharing Polly with the woman who'd reunited them. When had deferring to her, instead of relying on her own judgement, ceased to be a lack of confidence in her own judgement and simply become a habit?

Too long ago, and it was a habit she needed to break. It was long past time she stood on her own two feet. It was a terrifying thought, yet her heart beat a little faster at the prospect and despite the argument she found herself smiling. Amy was right—as always. That must have been some kiss. It had, without doubt, jarred something loose in her brain.

Not before time.

'Penny for them,' Jake said as he lay back in bed, watching Amy as she brushed out her hair.

'What?'

'Your thoughts. You've been lost in them ever since you called in on Kay.'

'Dominic Ravenscar is home,' she said, putting down the brush and swivelling on the stool to face him. 'He's asked Kay to do some work on the garden for him.'

'Well, that's good. Isn't it?'

'I handled it very badly. We very nearly had a row about it.'

Jake didn't ask what about. He knew his wife well

enough to understand that if she was concerned, there was something to be concerned about.

'Nearly?'

'I was insensitive. She got all prickly.'

'That doesn't sound like either of you.'

'No. I suddenly found myself remembering that time when George wanted you to take the training wheels off his bike.'

'And you said he'd fall off and hurt himself.'

'I was right. He did.'

'Freedom, independence, comes at a price.'

'She's going to do more than graze her knee, bang her elbow, Jake. He's going to break her heart.'

'Ravenscar? Why would he do that?'

'Oh, not deliberately. But he's still grieving and she thinks it's her duty to help him. Because we helped her.'

'Maybe she needs to prove something to herself. Or to you.'

'There's only one way a woman can help a man in such pain. He won't be able to resist that kind of giving, but afterwards he'll hate himself for it. Then he'll hate her.'

'Do you remember what people said when we looked for Kay? Brought her home?'

'That we were fools,' she said. 'That she wouldn't thank us—and she didn't. That we'd be sorry.' She palmed a tear from her cheek. 'There were times, Jake...'

'I know.' He got up, lifted her from the stool and held her close. 'I know, sweetheart,' he murmured into her hair. 'But you stuck with it and you did a good job. Don't underestimate her ability to survive. And don't underestimate yourself. If she's prepared to go out on a limb for him, it's only because you've made her strong enough to take the risk.'

She lifted her head to look up at him. 'What you're saying is that all I can do now is stand back and wait for the crash? Be ready to pick up the pieces? Again.'

'What I'm saying is that you should come to bed. It's been a long day and you've got a board meeting tomorrow...'

She waved that away as unimportant. 'You don't understand, Jake. What about Polly? She's the one who'll suffer—'

'Kay lives for Polly.'

'But—'

'She's *her* daughter. *Her* responsibility.'

'No—'

'Yes, Amy!' Then more gently, as she collapsed against his shoulder, 'I'm sorry, my love. I know how much you wanted a little girl of your own.'

'I've got three wonderful boys. I've got you.' She blinked back a tear, found a smile from somewhere. 'I think there's probably a rule that no one should have everything they want. That it's bad for us, or something...'

'Maybe it is. But that doesn't mean we shouldn't stop striving for it.' He bent to kiss her softly on the mouth, then said, 'Come to bed.'

Kay stood in front of the door set into Dominic Ravenscar's garden wall, feeling even more nervous than the first time she'd breached his defences. Which was ridiculous. This wasn't some clandestine raid on his blackberries. Nor was she standing here in some blind response to over-active hormones, as Amy had implied. This was just a job.

No. Scratch that. It wasn't *just* a job. It was a seriously well-paying one. And, having spent most of the night with a calculator, confronting the realities of life in the real world, she had better stow the nerves and get on with it.

This time she was expected. Invited. Commanded, even.

Unless, of course, he'd done what she advised—slept on his offer and sensibly changed his mind, was even now consulting with one of the big landscape-gardening companies in Maybridge. She couldn't believe how much she hoped he wasn't doing that. How important this job had become to her. What kind of an idiot was she to even suggest he do such a thing?

She wiped clammy palms down the seat of her work trousers and seized the handle. The only certainty was that she wouldn't learn what he'd decided to do out here in the lane.

She opened the gate, half expecting to see him standing there, waiting for her with that careful, unreadable expression blanking every emotion, every feeling from his face. She braced herself for him to be standing there, with what she hoped was a businesslike expression on her face. Whatever that was.

But the garden was empty.

The only indication that Ravenscar had ever been there was the For Sale sign lying face down in the grass, which presumably meant that he was serious about taking the house off the market.

Which was good, she told herself, burying the tiny flicker of disappointment deep. He wasn't here. He'd implied he might not be. Said that she should just start work. Fine. She swallowed. Fine. Then she grinned. If he wasn't here, it meant he hadn't changed his mind!

'Yes!' she said. Then, louder, 'Yes!'

And it would be a lot easier to get on with it without him standing at her shoulder, watching her every move. What she needed was a plan of action. A programme of work. And, using the only tools she'd brought with her, she began to tour the garden, making sketches, notes.

Dominic watched her from the first-floor window as she moved about the garden, making notes in a small loose-leaf notebook. She hadn't brought any tools, but it would appear that she'd decided to take the job if it was still on offer.

She'd advised him to sleep on it. Well, he hadn't slept much—he'd got out of the habit—but instead had spent a restless night wondering if she was right and he was making a huge mistake in persuading her to take on the garden. Not because he didn't believe she was the right person for the job, he knew she was. He just wasn't sure he could cope with her presence.

But it was all right. Today he had no trouble in separating fact from fantasy. What truly amazed him was that he'd ever been fooled.

'What are you doing, Miss Lovell? Or do you prefer Ms?'

'Miss is fine.' Kay, every nerve strained to catch a sound out of place, hadn't been fooled by the rustle of dead grass a second time. She glanced up from her notebook. 'And, since you asked me to bring my tools and start work straight away, Mr Ravenscar, that's what I'm doing.'

'I had something rather more practical in mind.'

'Not all gardening is done with the spade. I'm making a rough plan of the garden. Working out what needs to be done and in what order. When I get home I'll be able to sort out a schedule of work.' She couldn't help adding, 'On my computer.'

'I don't need a pen, or a computer, to tell you that the first job is to get the grass cut back.'

So much for congratulating herself that she wasn't going to get any interference.

'The mower is in the shed,' he added, as if she didn't know.

'I found it, thanks.'

He lifted a brow. 'Are you telling me that you broke that lock, too?'

CHAPTER FIVE

"The seasons alter: hoary-headed frosts
Fall in the fresh lap of the crimson rose."
William Shakespeare

KAY REGARDED him dispassionately. It wasn't easy. He had the kind of cheek bones, well-defined jaw that turned men into movie idols. The fact that the flesh was pared to the bone and a touch of silver was threaded through his dark hair did absolutely nothing to lessen his appeal. 'The lock was hanging off the door. I'll bring a new padlock tomorrow, but you might want to give some thought to upgrading your security.'

'What is this? You break into my garden and then sell me locks?'

'I'm the local neighbourhood-watch coordinator. I'll get the crime-prevention officer to call in and talk to you. Meantime,' she said, firmly changing the subject, 'I've called the local agents for your mower. They're going to pick it up in the morning and take it in for a service. And whatever else needs doing. Don't worry about waiting for them. I'll see them in. I can fix the lock at the same time.'

'You won't be working in the village shop?'

'Monday, Thursday and Friday mornings,' she said.

'Then—'

'No need to thank me,' she said, briskly, before he could finish. 'It's all part of the job. I'd do the same for you if you'd been lying in a damp shed for six years and were covered with dust and cobwebs.' She suddenly found herself unable to meet his gaze. It sounded too much like her original plan. Dust him off, rub him down, apply oil and he'd soon be ticking over nicely. She tried very hard not to think about applying the oil...

It wasn't going to be that easy.

Besides, this job was too important to her to risk messing it up by getting emotionally involved. She might not have liked what Amy had to say, but it didn't mean she hadn't taken the message aboard.

'Not that we'll be able to use it on this,' she went on, quickly covering an overlong silence and pointing her pen at the long, matted grass. 'I'll have Jim Bates call round with his scythe and take it down.'

'Jim Bates?'

'The verger. He keeps the churchyard tidy, bless him, and since handling a scythe is a skill I haven't yet mastered—' largely because she was scared witless that she'd chop her own feet off '—he does the odd job for me. Actually, I'll have him dig over the vegetable garden, too. He's steady, but he'll do a good job. Don't worry about paying him. I'll invoice you for his time. At cost,' she added, quickly in case he thought she would be making a profit on the deal. 'Well, maybe you could buy him a pint when you see him in the pub. I know he'd appreciate that.'

He didn't answer for a moment. Only when the silence had lasted a full thirty seconds did he say, 'Is that it? You've finished?'

'Yes.' Then, 'I'm so sorry. You were going to say something when I interrupted. Maybe you have a better idea?'

He glared at her. 'Just get on with it.'

'Absolutely.'

'And that includes buying Mr Bates a pint of ale. You can add that to the bill, too.'

'Oh, but…' She might not be prepared to get emotionally involved, but it had seemed like too good an opportunity to get him into the pub to miss. Get him into company. Which had to be a good thing. But he'd already turned away and was striding back towards the house.

And she hadn't finished.

'Mr Ravenscar…' she called. Oh, yuck. Why did she have to keep on calling him Mr? It sounded so hideously cringe-makingly below-stairs. Apart from Dominic Ravenscar she hadn't called any man ''Mr'' since the headmaster had invited her to vacate the sacred portals of his precious sixth form when he'd discovered that her ''upset stomach'' had less to do with a dodgy sandwich from the school refectory and more to do with the fact that she was pregnant. But it was too late to regret not sticking to ''Dominic'' now.

He didn't stop and she was forced to follow him, only catching up with him at the French windows.

'Mr Ravenscar, I—'

'What?' he demanded, turning on her.

She quailed beneath the ferocity of his frown. Wished she'd stayed at the far end of the garden. Too late now. He was waiting.

'I just wondered if Mrs Ravenscar kept a diary?'

'A diary?' he enquired, his voice like flint. 'And if she did? What possible business of yours could it be?'

What? 'Oh…no!' She shook her head. 'I didn't mean a personal one.' His face remained set in stone. 'I, um, meant a gardening diary. I keep one—well, two, actually. One for my own garden and one for clients. Weather, planting, crops. Jobs done. Jobs to do. Cuttings to trade. Seed catalogues to order.' Which was almost certainly more than he wanted to know. 'Anything and everything,' she added.

'I see.'

'Well does...did she?'

'Is it important?'

'It would help to know what exactly she was doing. Her vision for the garden. Not everything has survived.' Her gesture took in the wide perennial border. 'There are gaps. Well, you can see that for yourself.'

He glanced around. 'I can't see any gaps.'

'You can't?'

'Quite the reverse.'

'Oh, I see what you mean.' He was obviously one of those men who couldn't tell his *Passiflora* from his elbow. 'And when I've got rid of the weeds so will you.'

'Maybe you should be getting on with it instead of wasting my time.'

'I'm sorry. I didn't realise I was keeping you from work.'

He caught her glance at the dust sheet still lying on the floor and his jaw tightened. 'You've caught me between visits from the cleaner.'

'Once a month, isn't it? Forgive me, but I don't think you can wait another two weeks.'

'Are you offering to take on the dusting as well, Miss Lovell? On top of the two hours a day you're sparing me? When you're not busy talking. Are you sure you can spare the time?'

She gritted her teeth—metaphorically—and refused to

rise to the bait. 'I was going to suggest Mrs Fuller. She doesn't work on a regular basis, but she occasionally takes on special jobs. I think this would come under that category, don't you?' Then, when she didn't get any response, 'OK, well, think about it.'

'Is that it?'

'Yes.' Then, 'No! Sorry. Look, if Mrs Ravenscar didn't keep a diary, she might have had a working design. Maybe a planting plan?' she prompted. 'I'd hate to start digging and suddenly find I'm chopping into precious bulbs.'

He looked sorely tempted to tell her to go away and never come back. Instead he said, 'You'd better come in.'

'What? Oh, right.' She kicked off her shoes and caught up with him at the far end of the big square hallway.

'Sara used this room,' he said, opening a door next to the kitchen. 'She wouldn't use the study at the front of the house because it didn't overlook the garden.'

'Well,' she said, 'it's…compact.'

'The estate agent referred to it as "the butler's pantry", but I think perhaps he was getting a bit carried away with the whole "gentleman's residence" thing.'

'They will do that,' she agreed as she stepped passed him, although the security bars at the window and a glimpse of green baize lining the cupboard shelves suggested that he was not far out. But the shelves that had once held precious china were now filled with gardening and cookery books and a small desk filled the space at the end of room. A notebook lay open, a fountain pen and some coloured pencils near at hand. There were postcards, photographs of gardens clipped from glossy magazines and notes attached to a corkboard. And a photograph of Dominic looking young, happy as he smiled at the woman taking the picture.

It tore at her heart.

The room looked as if it was waiting. As if the occupant had just gone to make a cup of tea and would be back at any moment. She looked back, but he seemed unwilling to join her in the cramped space.

'Can I look around?'

'Help…yourself…' The words sounded as if they'd been squeezed from him.

She picked up the notebook. Unlike her own utilitarian notebooks, it was covered in cloth that shimmered like a peacock's feather and the handwriting was equally elegant, in keeping with the expensive pen Sara Ravenscar had used. As she turned the heavy, unlined pages, she realised the contents matched the exterior. This was far more than the basic working diaries she kept, with their occasional smudges of mud, but a record of everything that happened in the garden. From the sighting of a hedgehog, to the unexpected appearance of bluebells at the far end of the orchard. She'd illustrated it, too, with exquisite pen sketches.

'Is that what you're looking for?'

She looked up. 'Oh, yes. Sorry. But there must be more. This is only a quarter used.'

'Try the drawer.'

She did so, but it didn't budge.

'The key must be there somewhere.' She opened a small box that contained paper-clips, drawing pins, a couple of rubber bands. Before she could sift through them, a beeping sound emerged from one of her pockets. Kay fished out a small alarm clock and turned it off.

'My watch battery died,' she said, when she saw his what-on-earth-have-I-let-myself-in-for expression. 'I have to go, it's three-fifteen. School's out in five minutes.'

'I remember. Your daughter comes first.'

'I did tell you. If you have a problem with that—'

'No. Absolutely not. Don't keep her waiting for you. I was only irritable about short hours because I wanted you to get the garden finished quickly.'

'I did say—'

'I know. You never stop "saying". Just go. I'll look for the key. Maybe the plans are in the desk, too.' He walked with her to the door. Then, 'If you're going to be spending any amount of time at home working on this, please keep a note of your hours so that you can invoice me.'

'Oh, no. That isn't necessary. What else would I do in the evening?' Once Polly was in bed.

'I can't advise you on that. Merely that you won't be in business for long if you don't value your time. You should have a standard contract that sets out that sort of thing. Ask your friends the Hallams. They're both successful in business. I'm sure they'll advise you.'

She knew what their advice would be. Forget it. Stop fooling herself...

'Think about it,' he said, abruptly, when she didn't answer, clearly wishing he hadn't bothered.

'I'll think about it,' she offered, 'if you'll promise to think about getting Dorothy Fuller in to give this place a going over.'

'What is this? Have you got the whole village paying you a commission for work? Forget gardening. You should set up your own little domestic agency.'

It was the ''little'' that irritated her. What was it about her that made everyone assume that she was incapable of doing something *big*? But she didn't let it show, just regarded him thoughtfully and said, 'I don't suppose you're in the market for some hand-knitted sweaters? Winter's coming and I know a couple of old ladies who can produce the kind of stuff that would sell for telephone numbers in Knightsbridge.'

'Haven't you got a child to collect? I'll open the gate first thing so that you can let in the lawn-mower people,' he said. 'And don't forget to add that time to your account, too.'

'I'll ask Dorothy to call and see you, then, shall I?'

'Goodbye, Miss Lovell.'

'Until tomorrow, Mr Ravenscar.'

Dominic watched as she ducked beneath a low branch of an old copper beech that dominated what had once been a perfect lawn and, as she bent, displayed a neat rear smeared with greenish dust from its encounter with the low wall where she'd sat for a while drawing a rough plan of the garden.

Waiting until he heard the thump of the gate, then realising that it was still unlocked, he followed her and bolted it.

After that, avoiding an immediate return to a house that would seem even emptier without her presence to fill it with chatter, he went to look in the shed, to see for himself what kind of condition the mower was in. A small ride-on machine that he'd bought not long after they'd moved in, it was indeed covered in cobwebs and dust except for a wide sweep where Kay Lovell had brushed against it as she'd checked it out. Cobwebs, dust and worse, no doubt, if the tools, rusting in their clips against the wall, were anything to go by.

He took down a trowel, rubbed his thumb over the surface. It came away red, leaving the surface pitted and scarred. As he replaced it, he wondered what Kay Lovell would have to say about that.

That she would have some pithy comment to make he didn't doubt, because she had plenty to say about everything else.

Irritating woman.

Kay saw the lawn mower safely off the premises, expecting Dominic to appear at her side at any moment with some dry comment about paying her to stand around doing nothing. Again. He was, however, noticeable only by his absence.

She'd had to force herself not to keep glancing towards the house, half hoping to see the French windows open and the man himself walking down what was beginning to be a noticeable track through the long grass towards her. Surprised how much she minded when they stayed firmly shut.

No, she chided herself as she let herself out of the garden. Everything was shut up, which meant he'd gone out, and that had to be good. He was spending far too much time alone.

She walked around to the front of the house and slipped the envelope she'd planned to hand to him in person through the letterbox. The old village houses had doors that fronted directly on to the street and she was already turning away when a car pulled up alongside her. The kind of car that men drooled over and girls dreamed of being swept away in. Expensive, fast, upholstered in leather-scented luxury. Several yards longer than was entirely necessary for the basic purpose of transport.

'What did you put through my door?' Dominic Ravenscar unfolded himself from the driving seat and joined her on the pavement. 'Have you changed your mind about the job?'

She dragged her gaze away from the car and, reminding herself that she was way too old to drool, turned to face her new client. It was no good. In a cashmere jacket, linen shirt and a pair of immaculately cut trousers, he would make anyone drool.

Then she said, 'If I'd changed my mind, I wouldn't put a note through the door, I'd tell you to your face.'

'Yes, of course you would. So? Don't keep me in suspense. Was it an invitation to the harvest supper? The new issue of the parish magazine hot off the press? A list of the latest "specials" at the village shop?'

'None of the above,' she said. 'I just came by to oversee the removal of the mower and thought I'd give you my contract at the same time.'

'Your contract?' It was pathetically gratifying to realise that she'd taken him by surprise. 'You didn't waste much time thinking about it.'

'Was I supposed to? Sorry, but it's a commodity in short supply.' Which was probably the worst thing she could have said; she really could do with an intensive course in "tact". 'In my life.' Then, 'Nice car,' she said, hoping to distract him. She made a gesture that measured its length. 'Very…'

'Black?' he offered, with an edge to his voice that suggested she was walking a very narrow line.

'Clean.'

She'd been about to say ''sexy'', and suspected that he knew it.

He very nearly smiled and she thought if she could get him to go the whole way it would be worth any amount of embarrassment.

'Since I'm staying for a while, I thought I'd better do something about transport.'

'Transport? That isn't ''transport''. A bus is transport. That is pure self-indulgence.'

'There's a bus service?' he said. He might as well have said ''mind your own business….''

Quite right.

'Regular as clockwork,' she assured him. 'Three times a day.'

'As often as that? If only you'd told me yesterday.' He turned away to open the front door and bent down to pick up the envelope she'd just pushed through the letterbox. 'You'd better come in.'

About to tell him that there was no hurry, she actually managed to stop her runaway mouth. It had occurred to Kay that if she really wanted to twist Dominic Ravenscar's arm over employing Dorothy Fuller—and he really needed someone like her to get the house straight, someone who wouldn't wait to be told what to do, but just get on with it—she'd better fulfil her part of the bargain and not only think about a contract, but also come up with one. And quickly.

It wouldn't be difficult. All she had to do was pick up the phone and Amy or Jake would, she was sure, be able to provide her with some kind of standard document. And a lot of sound advice. All of it tempered with the ''Are you sure you can do this…?'' undertone that she wasn't in the mood to listen to.

It was time to stand on her own two feet. Metaphorically, if not legally, speaking. Whilst she was perfectly well aware that she knew as much about the law as Dominic knew about gardening, one of her OAPs had a son who was a lawyer. Mowing his mum's grass— so he didn't have to leave his busy life in London and do it himself—had to be worth a few minutes of his time, she figured. He clearly thought so, too. He'd not only emailed her a suitable document, with blanks for her to fill in her own details before she printed it off, he'd also spent some time on the phone going through her legal responsibilities. Making sure she had appropriate insurance. Encouraging her to think bigger. Get a proper name for her company. An image. And he'd promised to find out what start-up grants were available for new businesses, too.

It had been refreshing to be taken so seriously.

He'd even wanted to pay her for mowing his mum's lawn, but she wouldn't hear of it. He was far more valuable to her as a source of free legal advice.

'How did you manage to organise it so quickly?' Dominic asked, lifting the flap of the envelope and taking out the document headed with her new logo—she'd had a busy night—and company name. Daisy Roots: tough, persistent…and rhyming slang for boots. The lawyer had *really* liked it.

'I took your advice,' she said, and when he looked up, 'I thought about it and I realised that you're right. I might have a very small business, but that doesn't mean I shouldn't have ambition. And be one hundred per cent professional.'

It also occurred to her that it would be easier to convince the estate agents that she would only work for a realistic hourly rate if she wasn't just Kay Lovell, occasionally jobbing gardener, working for herself. She'd had a lot of fun producing her own letterheads, business cards and a pile of leaflets she'd left at the local gardening centre earlier that morning. She'd put enough business their way, after all.

'There are two copies,' she said. 'You just have to sign them both on the dotted line and give one back to me.'

'Is that all? Haven't you missed out the most important bit?' When she frowned. 'The bit about reading it first?'

'Oh, that's all right,' she said. 'I've already read it.' Then she grinned.

No! Not professional…

She pulled her face back into line and said, 'Sorry, very bad joke. Take your time. I'll pick it up this afternoon.' Then, because she didn't want to appear too pushy…she was new at this ''professional'' lark… 'Or whenever.'

'It won't take that long,' he said as she stepped back and turned to leave. He opened the door wider. 'Why don't we get it over with? Unless you have to rush off to some other job.'

Well, there was a pile of ironing that never seemed to get any smaller. She had promised to catalogue the resource materials for the village school before half-term, too. And there was Polly's birthday party to plan. That was going to be a surprise, so she'd have to do it all during the day…

But she suspected he meant a real job. The kind that paid money.

'I'll allow you to make us both a cup of coffee while I read it,' he persisted.

'Oh, right.' Professional? Who did she think she was kidding? 'Who could possibly resist an offer like that?'

Dominic didn't want her to go.

He hadn't admitted it to himself at the time, but he'd gone out this morning to avoid seeing her. Not because she reminded him of Sara, but because she reminded him that he was a man.

Coming back and seeing her on his doorstep dressed in unflattering working clothes, a dusty cobweb that she must have picked up in the tool shed clinging to her hair and without a scrap of make-up on her face, didn't appear to make a blind bit of difference.

There was something refreshing about her. Totally natural. She constantly put her foot in her mouth, but when she did she laughed, or blushed, or looked momentarily distraught. But she didn't quit. She just took it out again and ploughed on. That was rare.

As a result, he'd probably talked to her more in two days than he had anyone of his acquaintance in the last six years. About anything but work, anyway.

'Maybe I can tempt you with the rest of Sara's notebooks?' he said, using the one thing that he knew she wouldn't be able to resist as a lure. 'I found her garden plan, too.'

It had actually been easier looking for something specific, rather than going through the depressing piles of old bills and papers, shredding them. Feeling guilt at the destruction of things that Sara had touched.

'Oh, well, now you're talking,' she said, and genuine pleasure lit up her face. 'For those, Mr Ravenscar, you get your coffee.'

Which certainly put her priorities in perspective.

'If I had an ego to dent,' he said, 'you'd be a major traffic accident.'

'No offence, but I've seen what you do with hot drinks,' she came back, not missing a beat. 'I've also read your wife's prose,' she went on, bending to unlace her boots and kick them off as she stepped inside. 'Frankly, there's no contest.'

She had a hole in one of her socks, he noticed. And found himself wondering how she managed to support herself and her little girl. Why they were alone. Or maybe they weren't. She hadn't mentioned anyone, he hadn't seen anyone at the cottage, but that didn't mean a thing. He could be away…

No. If there had been someone in her life she wouldn't have responded to his kiss with quite that hunger. Quite that warmth.

'Your wife was a gifted communicator,' she said, straightening. She was taller than Sara. Even in her socks she very nearly looked him in the eye. Maybe that was what made it so impossible to ignore her. She looked him in the eye and wasn't afraid to hold his gaze. 'Her enthusiasm made the garden really come alive for me. Reading her notebook made me feel as if I knew her. I can see why you miss her so much.'

Miss her? For a moment, just a moment, he'd forgotten…

'I'll put on the kettle,' he said, abruptly. 'You'll find everything in her study.'

Dismissed, Kay found herself staring at his back as he walked away from her. What had she said? One moment he'd been close to teasing her, the next…bang. The shutters came slamming back down. It was like walking on eggshells. But then, as she was the first to admit, she had big feet.

She really should learn to keep her opinions to herself, stick to what she knew something about. Like weeding.

She put the notebooks to one side to study later and opened up the plan. It was perfect. Beautifully drawn and coloured, with the botanical names of the plants written in perfect copperplate script.

She was still admiring it when Dominic placed a mug beside her.

'Oh, sorry!' Her hand flew to her mouth. 'I forgot all about making coffee.'

He leaned back against the desk, cradling his own mug, while she drank hers. 'No problem. I should be the one apologising. Again.'

'Why?'

'I suppose I don't really know how to cope when people mention Sara.' He shrugged. 'I haven't had that much practice. After she died most of our friends would have rather stuck hot needles in their eyes than talk about her.'

She glanced at him over the rim of the mug. 'If you're that touchy I can see why.'

No, no, no! She'd just crawl under the desk and extract her size nines from her mouth.

But he was staring into his coffee as if, in its depths, he might find some kind of answer and for a moment she didn't think he'd heard her. Then he looked up. 'Despite recent evidence to the contrary, it's not because I snap their heads off. Unlike you, most people wouldn't give me a chance to talk about her after she died. Now, well, it would seem I've forgotten how to.'

'I'm sorry. It must have been very hard for you.'

'They meant well. I imagine they believed that if they didn't say her name I might manage to forget her more quickly.'

'Are you sure about that?'

'What other reason could there be for trying to wipe out all memory of her? To act as if she had never existed?' He shrugged, drawing attention to his shoulders; he was spare, lean to the bone, and the fine linen shirt he wore hung from them, but his frame was still impressive. 'All I got were offers to come and take her clothes away. Brush her life under the carpet as quickly as possible. Move on.' He grimaced. 'That was an expression I heard a lot of.'

'Maybe they were hoping that if there weren't constant reminders everywhere you looked, it would be easier for you to forget the pain,' she pointed out gently. 'They were wrong, of course. You need to talk about her. That way you can remember the joy. Going away wasn't the answer.'

'Are you sure you don't mean running away?' His eyes were slate in a chalk-white face.

'There's more than one way of doing that, but it's only a holding measure. Sooner or later you have to deal with it face to face.'

CHAPTER SIX

"Here's flowers for you:
Hot lavender, mints, savory, marjoram."
                              William Shakespeare

OH, GREAT. There she went again. Coming over all psychological. And, despite a few difficult moments, she thought she'd been doing quite well. She didn't wait for the explosion but put down the mug and turned her attention back to the plan, as if she hadn't just tossed off a metaphorical hand grenade.

'And one of the things you're going to have to deal with is the summer house, I'm afraid,' she said. 'It's a real shame; it must have been beautiful in its heyday. But unfortunately it's got a severe case of *decrepitus*.'

'What?' He seemed to come back from somewhere a long way distant. 'Is that some kind of fungus?' Then he realised what she'd said and managed to find something that was almost a smile from somewhere. It was almost painful to see. 'Oh, I see. That was another of your jokes, wasn't it?'

'Very nearly,' she admitted. 'I've been trying to give them up. I'm down to five a day.' Then, 'Well, maybe not *every* day...'

The "almost smile" was pumped up to something that was scarcely distinguishable from the real thing unless you were really looking. And she was really looking. It almost broke her heart to see him making the effort for her and she wanted to take his hand, put her arms around him and tell him that she understood. That it would be all right. That one day it would be all right. She resisted the temptation. Whatever his reaction—whether he hugged her back, or recoiled in horror—it could only result in terminal embarrassment.

'Please, don't feel you have to laugh,' she said. 'It isn't in the least bit compulsory.'

'OK.' And without warning deep lines fanned out from his eyes and the smile became the real thing.

'I suspect it's only the clematis that's holding it up,' she said, catching her breath, forcing herself to concentrate on the job in hand. 'Which is only fair, since it caused the problem in the first place. That's very old, too. It may even have been planted when the summer house was first put up. I imagine it seemed like a good idea at the time.'

'I remember Sara saying that it would have to be cut back hard, but she was waiting for it to flower first just in case…'

His voice trailed away, and to cover the sudden silence she said, 'I can just see it from Polly's window and it does look an absolute picture.'

'The first flowers opened on the day of her funeral.'

Kay swallowed. What was that about eggshells? A minefield was more like it. An unmarked minefield…

'I picked some to lay beside her, so that she would see them, but the petals dropped.'

'"…You seize the flow'r, its bloom is shed…"' she murmured. Then blushed as he stared at her. 'It's from a poem, I think,' she said. 'I, um, saw it on a calendar.'

'"But pleasures are like poppies spread, You seize the flow'r, its bloom is shed…" It's by Robert Burns.' This time the silence seemed endless and she had no words to fill it. Dominic Ravenscar did it for her. 'What happened to Polly's father?'

The abrupt change of subject threw her and she responded to this unexpected jab at a raw nerve in much the same way as he had. Instinctively. Defensively.

'Polly never had a father.'

Her only excuse was that it had been a long time since anyone had asked her that question. Maybe, like him, she had erected some kind of warning signal over her own emotional no-go area. Or perhaps she'd blotted it out so thoroughly that she'd stopped noticing the way people tiptoed around the subject. Whatever it was, she just wasn't prepared.

Ashamed of her instinctive reaction, her need to protect her own feelings, she tried again. 'I... That is, he...'

It wasn't usually this much of a problem. But then her standard answer—''He was young—he needed to find himself. He's still looking...''—was calculated to make people laugh, give her an opportunity to change the subject. What was that she'd said about there being more than one way to run?

He shifted, put down the mug. 'OK, what do you suggest?'

'Suggest?' she repeated, confused. What on earth did that mean? Then, belatedly, she realised that he was the one who'd changed the subject, rescuing her as she floundered, lost for an explanation that wouldn't leave her stripped bare, exposed. She realised that she'd allowed her unresolved issues to stand in the way of a precious opportunity to help him open up, talk about his. And now she'd missed her moment. Failed him at the first real chance that had presented itself.

Maybe it wasn't too late. Maybe if she could just find the words she could go back—

'You're the professional,' he said as, taking his cue from her hesitation and taking a quick step back from the personal, he returned the conversation firmly to business. And the moment was gone. Lost beyond recall. 'So what's your professional opinion?'

She'd gathered herself, promised herself she'd find some way to put it right. Soon. In the meantime, all she could do was concentrate on the matter in hand. Which was...

'Oh, yes. Well, I had a look at it this morning while I was waiting for the lawn-mower people,' she said. 'It's beyond saving, I'm afraid.'

'The summer house?'

'The clematis.' Then, 'Well, both of them.'

This comment was met by a silence and for an endless moment she held her breath, conscious that she'd just ridden roughshod over what must be pretty raw feelings. How could she be so insensitive?

'I could try cutting it back,' she offered. 'If you'd prefer that. It might recover.'

'Sara clearly thought it would.'

'Sara wasn't going to pull down the summer house.' She left it at that. His decision. She'd do her best, either way.

There was another long pause. Then, apparently coming to a decision, he said, 'No. We should replace it. Them. A new summer house and a new climber. Something special.'

We?

Her heart, which had apparently stopped beating while she waited for him to tell her to go and never darken his door again for daring to suggest hacking down something so precious, did a wild pirouette before galloping to catch up.

'Right. I'll, um...' She cleared her throat, made a point of folding up the plan so that she could avoid looking at him. 'I'll have a look on the 'net for suppliers, if you like. Get some catalogues.'

'Are you telling me that you don't know some man in the village who could design and build a replacement in his spare time?'

What? She glanced up, caught a glint of something that looked disturbingly like mischief lifting the corner of his mouth. He was teasing her?

'Well, overlooking the sexist notion that it would take a man...'—it took considerable effort to keep her own face resolutely straight—'I suppose next time I was mowing his lawn I could ask Mark Hilliard if he'd like to dash you off one of his award-winning designs. Or you could come to the harvest supper and ask him yourself.'

'Hilliard? The architect?'

She thought that he was avoiding the invitation, rather than confirming the identity of his illustrious neighbour, but she obliged him.

'He lives in the Old Rectory. On the other side of the green.'

'That's...handy. But does he do rural rustic?'

'Well, no. Not usually. But I bet he'd design you something absolutely stunning in glass and steel.' Then, when his eyebrows shot up, 'Just kidding.'

'So was I.'

'No, you were mocking. There is a difference. I realise

that Upper Haughton must seem a bit quaint after travelling the world—'

'No, I'm sorry. It's a lot more than that. We moved here in the first place because it was the kind of place that people care about one another. Where there's always someone who knows someone who could do exactly what you need at that very moment. Where giving a neighbour a pot of your prize-winning home-made jam is as natural as breathing.'

'To be honest, with the jam it's just showing off,' she said. 'We're neighbourly, but I promise you we can be as gossipy and small-minded as the next place when we want to be.'

'Don't disillusion me.'

For a moment they seemed to hover on the edge of something. Possibilities hung in the air waiting to be put into words that neither of them seemed able to summon up. Then he said, 'Maybe you'd like to give some thought to a suitable climber?'

'Me?' She was deeply touched that he would ask her and without thinking she reached out and touched his hand. 'Thank you.'

He looked down, then up into her eyes.

She carefully withdrew her hand. Cleared her throat. Of course he'd ask her. Who else would he ask? He clearly didn't know ''Nelly Moser'' from Nelly the Elephant. It didn't mean anything.

'I'll do some research, Mr Ravenscar. Find some suitable candidates for you to choose from.' Then, 'It's quite possible that Sara had already given some thought to the matter. Clematis are tricky and she must have known that hacking back the *montana* might have proved terminal. She hasn't put anything on the plan, but I'm sure she'd have thought about it. Made notes in her journal. Can I take the rest of the books home with me?' She had to get out of that tiny room so that she could breathe. 'Or maybe you'd rather look through them yourself?'

'No,' he said, in a voice that seemed hazed with emotion. But while he was thinking about his poor dead wife, her thoughts had taken an altogether earthier turn. She felt scorched by that brief touch. Inflamed by the nearness of him. 'You need them more than I do at the moment.' Then, more forcefully, 'Don't forget to make a note of the time you spend reading them.'

Which was the verbal equivalent of a bucket of cold water.

'Don't worry, I've had advice from a lawyer. He took the time to explain all about charging for every minute. Every phone call. Every letter,' she said, hurt that he was still dragging money into their relationship. OK, so it was a business relationship, but even so...

'Can you afford someone who charges by the minute on your hourly rate?' he asked with an edge to his voice, suggesting that he'd got the message.

'We used the country method of invoicing. It cuts down on the book-keeping.' She dredged up a grin—it felt more like a grimace from where she was standing— and plastered it on her face. 'He gave me half an hour of his time and in return I mow his mother's lawn.'

'How long for?' he demanded, horrified.

'As long as she needs me to, but then I'd do it anyway, so to all intents and purposes I get his time for free. You needn't worry, though, gardening is different to practising law—I don't charge by the minute. Besides,' she added, glancing down at the pile of notebooks, more to avoid looking at him than to reacquaint herself with the peacock covers, 'reading these isn't work, it's a pleasure.'

'Let's argue about that at the end of the month when you submit your account. In the meantime, here's your contract, duly signed, Miss Lovell,' he said, extracting the folded document from the pocket of his shirt and handing it to her. And they were back on an even keel again, after a stormy few minutes.

Maybe they'd even moved forward a little. At least he'd moved forward a little; she needed to be on her own to work out where she was. But at least he now trusted her with more than his weeds. She placed the contract on top of the plan and notebooks and gathered them up in her arms, holding them against her chest.

'I'll see you this afternoon,' she said, as she headed for the front door and he opened it for her. 'That's if you'll be here?' She glanced at the car standing in front of the house as she pushed her feet into her boots. Then looked around helplessly for somewhere to set down her burden while she did up her laces.

'Here, let me,' he said as, seeing her difficulty as she struggled to control the pile of books, he retrieved them before they shot everywhere. Their fingers momentarily collided, his hand brushed against her breasts so that she was glad to stoop and take her time doing up her boots, giving her quick blush time to fade.

When she straightened he held out the books so that she could take them—very carefully—and said, 'I have no plans to be anywhere else this afternoon.'

'Excellent,' she said, not quite able to meet his gaze. 'In that case I'll bring Dorothy Fuller with me and she'll tell you what needs doing in the house.'

It was possible that he said something. Under his breath. She didn't ask him to repeat it.

Kay scarcely noticed the walk home. Someone spoke to her and she replied, but could not have said who, or what was said. Only that a few minutes later she found herself at her gate.

How was it that after a really intense kiss she'd felt safe enough, sufficiently in control to contemplate working for Dominic Ravenscar, yet that single touch to his hand had felt like the most dangerous thing she'd ever done?

Even now, the tips of her fingers tingled and she curled them hard against the palm of her hand in a vain attempt to put a stop to the disturbing sensation before it spread up her arm and escaped into the rest of her body. Tingling like that could cause total havoc in a confined space. Such as the heart.

Amy had tried to warn her that the situation was explosive; if she hadn't gone quite so far as to declare that it would all end in tears, her restrained silence had been a master class in eloquence.

But had she been listening? No. Well, yes…but all she'd heard was the doubt in Amy's voice. Or had it been fear that she'd get hurt? Or, worse, that Polly might suffer from any emotional backlash? She had every right…

She'd just have to be more careful in future. No touching. Not even thinking about touching. Definitely no *tingling*.

She'd just get on with the job, work at getting her fledgling business off the ground and into the air. And she'd be herself. A good neighbour. Maybe that would be enough.

Kay's confused train of thought was distracted by a basket tucked under the bench in her back porch. She put Sara Ravenscar's notebooks on the bench and pulled it out.

There was an envelope tucked into the handle, but she didn't need a note to tell her who had left it. It was one of the expensive gift baskets from the "Amaryllis Jones" aromatherapy range, produced by Amy's company and sold in the chain of shops she controlled. Although she always went to London on a Monday, she'd still found the time to call and make her peace...

She withdrew the card and read, "Kay, darling, you might find these useful. With love, Amy."

Useful?

Opening the basket, she saw that it wasn't an off-the-shelf package with pampering creams and soaps, but a rather more workmanlike range of essential oils. She picked one of them out of the basket. Bergamot. Like all the citrus oils, it was uplifting, alleviated depression. She knew that much. There was camomile, too. And rose absolute, one of Amy's favourites. She used it to relieve emotional distress. Had used it on her...

Useful.

'Oh, I see,' she said. Clever Amy. Kind Amy. This wasn't a simple peace offering, but a purely practical gift. A reminder that if she wanted to help Dominic, she should be thinking laterally.

How she was going to use it to help him was another matter entirely. She didn't think that anything as direct as offering him a massage would be well received. Not that she'd ever given anyone a massage, but she could just imagine stroking her hands gently over his back, down his spine...

She realised the tingling was getting out of hand and forced herself to stop. *No tingling!*

She'd need to be subtler in her approach.

It needed some thought, she decided, looking to see what else the basket contained.

Lavender. Was there anything that lavender wasn't good for? And marjoram. She frowned. Amy had given her a book on oils once, in an attempt to redirect her interest from the horticultural course she was determined on, hoping to draw her into the business, but she'd stubbornly resisted the easy option. Even then, she'd known she needed to find her own way.

But she'd read the book and there was something about marjoram that jangled in her memory. Something about the ancient Egyptians. She gathered everything up and went indoors to look it up.

Yes, that was it.

The ancient Egyptians had used it as a palliative for grief.

There was a tang of autumn in the air. Wood smoke. The mournful scent of Michaelmas daisies. There had been an early touch of frost when he'd woken that morning. It was gone at the first touch of sun, but it was a warning that the year was beginning the slow wind down to winter.

Dominic didn't have a problem with that. Winter didn't bother him. It was spring, the over-the-top rush of blossom with its promise of new life that shrivelled his heart.

As he crossed the lawn to the summer house to take

a better look, he could see that Kay Lovell was right.
From a distance, or if you weren't looking too hard—
afraid of what you might see—the decay looked merely
picturesque. Up close the picture was a great deal more
depressing. Unchecked, the climber had pushed its way
through the tiniest chinks in the timber of the summer
house, forcing it apart, and once the rain had got in nothing could save it, or the upholstered bamboo chairs and
sofa still inside, which on closer inspection he saw were
covered in green mould.

If he'd been here, he might have stopped it—he tested
the base with his foot and there was an ominous creak—
but it was too late now. He stepped back, glancing up.
But nothing moved except a small bird that erupted from
the tangled climber. Even so, the sooner it was demol-
ished the better. He had no doubt that Kay knew someone who could do the job for him. And probably someone else to provide a skip to bear away the remains as
well. At this rate, he'd have employed half the village
by the time the garden was restored.

He turned as he heard the gate open, glanced at his
watch. It was too early for her to be starting work and
it occurred to him that a simple bolt was not exactly the
most sensible security arrangement—not when he had to
leave it drawn for most of the day.

But it wasn't an intruder this time. He heard the soft
murmur of Kay's voice, but when, with a lift of the heart
that set it pounding just a little faster, he walked around
the summer house he saw that she was not alone.

'Miss Lovell. Again,' he said. She appeared somewhat
flustered at his appearance, he thought. As disturbed as
he was by hers. Thankfully, he was the one who didn't

blush. 'You certainly live up to your new company name.'

She drew her brows together in puzzlement. 'Daisy Roots?'

'Just so. No matter how hard you try to get rid of them, they just keep coming back.' Of course, he had just signed a contract with her, so he wasn't trying that hard...

She looked at her wrist, then, belatedly remembering that her watch was out of action, lifted her shoulders in the smallest of shrugs. 'I'm a little early, that's all. It wasn't my intention to disturb you—'

'No?' Then she was failing miserably. She'd disturbed him the evening he returned home and she'd been doing it ever since in one way or another.

'—but some things just won't wait.'

She gave him an unexpectedly cool glance, which was easier to deal with than her blushes. But not much.

'Actually, I thought you'd be too busy to notice I was here,' she said. 'Doing whatever it is you're doing.'

And the wretched woman cocked a brow at him, as if to suggest it wasn't much.

'I've made a start.' He had half a sack of shredded paper, magazines so yellow with age and so out of date that they wouldn't be welcome even in a dentist's waiting room. But it didn't take much to distract him. He was making a lifetime career out of avoiding what had to be done. 'Now I've stopped for lunch,' he lied. 'And a little fresh air.'

'It is a little musty in there,' she agreed, 'but Dorothy will be here just after three. Be nice to her and she'll have the house smelling sweet again in no time.'

He refused to commit himself to being ''nice'', but

instead looked down at the large shallow basket she was carrying. 'What have you got there?' He was something of a master at changing the subject, too.

'Herbs. These are lemon thyme,' she said, indicating a dozen or so small pots. 'And this,' she said, breaking off a stem from a much larger plant, 'is marjoram.' She rubbed the leaves and held it up for him to smell. The clean, sharp scent was surprisingly pungent, but it was her hand that held his attention. Her neat nails. The scratch where the bramble had caught her. It wasn't a pampered hand, but she'd laid it over his in a gesture of comfort that he could still feel.

Except that what he'd felt hadn't been comfort. Then or now.

He'd fooled himself into believing he was employing her simply because she was the right person for the job. Promised her that if she took it, she'd be quite safe from his unwanted attentions. What would she do if he took it now, pulled her close and kissed her again?

'It's rather strong,' he said, discouragingly.

'Don't worry—' she handed him the crushed leaves, smiling absently when he took them from her '—I'm not going to charge you for them. I grew a load of them from cuttings for the summer fête. Too many. These come under the heading of a neighbourly gesture.'

He wasn't going there again. 'I haven't got a herb garden.' Then, 'Have I?'

'According to the plan, there's one buried somewhere under the weeds. Or maybe Sara didn't get that far?'

He shook his head, realised he had no idea. 'The garden was her territory. I had a business to run.'

She waited, but when he didn't elaborate she said, 'It doesn't matter. I've got other plans for these. I thought we might plant the lemon thyme between the paving stones on the terrace. When I've cleared the weeds. It smells wonderful when you brush against it as you walk by.'

He thought she might repeat the gesture so that he could smell them for himself, but she didn't.

'Isn't there a lot to do before you start thinking about planting anything?' he said.

'It's never too early to start thinking about it. And when the work is hard—and this will be hard—it's good to have something to look forward to.' Then, 'Do you know Jim Bates?' she said, placing the basket on the veranda of the summer house and turning to introduce her companion. And it occurred to him that he was not the only one skilful at changing the subject.

It gave him the uneasy feeling that she was up to something.

But what?

He offered the man his hand. 'I recognise the face,' he said, telling himself that he was imagining things. Not for the first time where Kay Lovell was concerned. 'Thank you for helping out, Jim. Are you going to make a start on the grass today?'

'Kay said it needed doing and I thought I'd best get it cut while the weather holds,' he said, and removed the sacking from the long, heavy blade.

Dom looked up at a cloudless sky. 'Is there some danger of rain?'

'Jim keeps a piece of seaweed by the back door,' Kay explained. 'It never fails.'

'That's right.' He made a couple of test passes with the scythe. 'And when I was listening to the long-range forecast on the radio last night the young lady said there was a weather front moving in from the west.' And with that, he headed off to the far end of the garden.

'Miss Lovell,' he said, turning back to face her, attempting to reclaim control. That was a mistake.

Looking at her.

It hadn't been just his body that had reacted when she'd touched him—thankfully she'd been looking up at his face so hadn't noticed just how eagerly it had reacted—but something deep inside him seemed to light up, too.

'Miss Lovell,' he repeated, as if by hanging on to some semblance of formality he could keep a lid on the havoc she was wreaking to a libido jarred disturbingly into life. It was the kiss, that was all. And that had been a mistake, he reminded himself. The result of an illusion… 'I was wondering if, amongst your many local contacts, you know anyone who would be interested in demolishing this for me?'

She glanced up at the summer house and then back at him.

'Of either sex,' he added, when she didn't immediately answer. And was repaid with a smile for his trouble. It lit up her eyes. Yes, they were grey, but now he could see they had flecks of amber, or maybe gold, in them that were picked up by the sun.

She didn't immediately answer him, but walked around the structure, taking her time about it, regarding it thoughtfully. Putting her foot to it and giving it a shove, as he had done earlier, and getting much the same result. When she had completed the circumnavigation, she finally said, 'No, I'm inclined to believe that on this occasion masculine muscle is all that's needed.'

'You mean that it's a job only a man can do?' he

pressed, enjoying her unexpected capitulation in the face of a little rotting timber.

Her smile suggested that wasn't exactly what she meant, but she didn't argue. On the contrary. 'Absolutely. And I know just the man. Don't go away. I'll be right back.'

CHAPTER SEVEN

"There's rosemary, that's for remembrance; pray, love, remember: and there is pansies, that's for thoughts."
William Shakespeare

'MISS LOVELL…Kay…' But before he could stop her, tell her that he hadn't meant now, this minute, she was halfway down the garden and out of sight behind the dense evergreen hedge that screened the kitchen garden from the house.

He assumed she was going to fetch some muscle-bound village youth with time on his hands and a talent for destruction that needed a suitable outlet, but when she returned almost immediately with another crop of cobwebs decorating her hair, a smear of dust on her cheek and carrying a heavy, long-handled sledgehammer, he knew he wasn't that lucky.

'Here you go,' she said, dropping the head on the ground at his feet, angling the handle in his direction so that he had no option but to take it from her. To say he wished he'd stayed inside was an understatement. Didn't she understand that to order the destruction of something full of sweet memories was hard enough? She couldn't expect him to do it himself.

She waited.

Clearly she could.

Forget staying inside…he was beginning to wish he'd never come home.

In the world's inhospitable places—in a worn-out truck pounding across the Sahara with nothing to bother him but the heat, the flies, the sand scouring his face, or hacking through some mosquito-infested swamp, wringing wet with humidity and sweat—there had been nothing but discomfort to remind him that he was alive. No one to force him to confront the fact, acknowledge that life went on.

His life, anyway, despite all efforts to put himself in harm's way.

But Kay Lovell seemed hell bent not just on reminding him, but forcing him to get on with it. None of that tentative "time to move on" stuff with her. The sledgehammer seemed entirely appropriate.

'You are really pushing your luck,' he said. 'You know that, don't you?'

She regarded him solemnly. 'I know that's a very expensive shirt you're wearing,' she said. 'I'd advise changing into something with a little less style and a little more substance before you get started. Something I'd better do myself,' she said, glancing at her wrist as if to check the time. 'I really must do something about my watch.' She turned as if to walk away, but then looked back. 'Would you mind moving that basket out of harm's way before you start? It's old but I'm fond of it. The terrace gets full sun; the plants will like it there until I can—'

'We have a contract, Miss Lovell. Under your terms of engagement, everything in the garden is your responsibility. You brought them here. You look after them. It is, after all, what I'm paying you for.'

She flinched at that but he was too angry to care. He

tossed the handle to the grass, angry with her for being right, angry with himself for getting into such a situation.

'Just…just get on with it,' he said.

That was tense. Kay held onto the railing for a moment, more shaken than she could have believed possible by that encounter.

It was always going to be difficult. She had never been good at acting, but the business with the marjoram had been carefully thought out and she'd rehearsed the moves in her own kitchen until she could break off a few leaves, bruise them before holding them up for him to smell as if it was the most natural thing in the world. Which it was.

Of course her hand hadn't shaken when she was trying it out on the cat. But then Mog's eyes hadn't been narrowed suspiciously at her. Unlike Dominic's, who certainly suspected she was up to something but, for the life of him, couldn't imagine what.

It didn't matter. What mattered was that the scent of marjoram would cling to his fingers, stay with him for a while. She'd achieved her objective. She just hoped the ancient Egyptians knew what they were talking about.

After that, though, she'd been playing it by ear.

She looked down at the hammer, then picked it up and laid it carefully on the summer-house veranda out of Jim's way.

Knocking down the summer house, a place that would be full of memories, would be tough. It would, she realised, be difficult for him even to ask someone else to do it.

Well, there was no rush.

Getting angry was a good sign. It had certainly knocked that contained, expressionless look out of his eyes. Dark they might be—slate-dark grey—but they'd sparked with fire for a moment there.

Meantime they had, as he'd just rather pointedly reminded her, a contract. It was time to stop trying to put the world to rights and start earning a living.

Dominic banged the French windows closed, shutting himself off from the garden, leaning back against them, as if to block any chance of her following him the way she had before. He stayed there while the pulse hammering in his throat quietened, his breathing returned to something like normal. Then he dragged his hands over his face, as if to rid himself of Kay Lovell.

A mistake. He was instantly assailed by the scent of the plant she'd offered him and which he'd stupidly taken. Sharp, fresh...

Damn it, he needed to stay away from Kay Lovell. She made him angry. Anger wasn't good. The only way to survive was to clamp down on that kind of uncontrolled, emotional reaction... He heard a noise behind him and turned despite himself.

She was just outside on the terrace on a small stepladder, cutting back the roses that had run wild there. Working from the house outwards.

As she reached up, her T-shirt rose up to reveal a strip of golden skin that gleamed like silk in the sun, begging to be touched.

He turned abruptly away. She made him angry, but worse, much worse, she stirred up feelings that he'd buried so deep he'd forgotten what they could do to a man.

'Why aren't you in the shop this morning?'

It had been nearly two weeks since the incident over

the summer house, and since he hadn't made any attempt to do anything about it—in fact he was pretty much avoiding her all together—Kay had decided to give him a reminder that he couldn't just ignore the problem and hope it would go away. Which was why she was pushing a pile of brochures she'd accumulated through the Linden Lodge letterbox, hoping to provoke some kind of reaction. Hoping he'd join her in the garden and go through the designs she'd marked as possible replacements.

It was not to be. The front door was flung open before she'd crossed the pavement to her aged van.

She turned slowly. It didn't help. The low, distinctive sound of his voice had already tugged at something deep within her and as she saw his lean figure framed in the doorway her heart lost its timing. But at least she'd taken the very necessary deep breath before turning around, which meant she could look him in the eye and, going for cool surprise, say, 'I'm sorry?'

And her voice hardly shook at all.

'It's Friday.'

'The day that follows Thursday,' she agreed. 'Every week.'

'It's one of your mornings in the shop,' he said, pointedly. 'But you weren't there earlier.'

'I'm still not there,' she said, surprised that he'd remember the mornings she worked. Or notice if she wasn't there. He'd come in a few times while she'd been working, but she'd been serving in the post office and he hadn't so much as glanced in her direction, let alone stopped to buy a stamp. 'I've had to cut back my hours,' she said. 'Did you want to talk to me? You could have called at the cottage.'

Or spoken to her when she'd seen him in The Feathers on quiz night, buying Jim Bates the drink he owed him. She'd been so surprised that she'd missed a question and had to be brought back to attention by Amy and Dorothy, neither of whom had noticed him. She'd applied herself to the quiz and when she'd looked again, he'd gone.

Or any afternoon while she was working. But he'd been noticeable only by his absence. She'd hoped he was busy clearing out the past, preparing for the future. Nothing that Dorothy had said, however, suggested that that was the case. And there hadn't been a pile of sacks to be picked up on the days the garbage truck made its collection.

'Business picking up?' he asked.

'Yes, it is. Thanks in the main to you. Look, I'm sorry, I can't stop and talk now, I'm on the way to the bank.' She made a vague gesture in the direction of the van and said, 'As you can see, if I'm going to make the right impression on potential clients, I need a transport upgrade.' She didn't add that she was relying on his contract to help swing a business loan. 'Why don't you have a look at those?' she said, nodding at the pile of glossy brochures at his feet. 'There are all shapes and sizes of garden buildings to choose from. If you need any help deciding I'll go through them with you this afternoon.'

'Wait,' he said, as she turned to open the van door. 'I'm going into town. We can talk on the way. We'll take my car.'

'Oh, but—'

'I insist,' he said, reaching for a jacket hanging over the newel post and pulling the door shut behind him.

'Really, this isn't...' She jumped as he placed his

hand at her back to direct her firmly towards his garage—once a stable block, it now housed mechanical horsepower instead of the real thing. Even through the light wool jacket, silk shirt and teddy, it seemed to burn her skin.

'My bag. My business plan...' she protested.

He paused, just long enough to retrieve them and hand them to her. She looked back at the van as if to safety. 'You didn't lock it. The keys are still in the ignition.'

'If you're lucky someone will steal it,' he replied, opening the door of his low, sleek sports car, easing her into the passenger seat without ever losing contact. 'But I wouldn't hold your breath.'

'No! I love that old crate,' she declared as the soft leather upholstery hugged her in ergonomic comfort. Dominic Ravenscar looked pretty sceptical. 'All right, *love* might be a bit strong—' especially on cold mornings when it refused to start without resort to brute force '—but I do need it. The bank is going to be hard enough to convince as it is, without telling them I need two new vans. New second-hand, that is. And it looks worse than it really is. It passed its road-worthy test only last month.'

'Two?'

He had a way of hacking through her words, no matter how many of them she threw at him, and picking out the important one.

'Wayne, one of the village lads, is going to do the contract mowing for me until the end of October. The routine stuff.'

'Is he reliable?'

'He did some gardening when he was on community service last year—'

'Community service? Oh, terrific. What did he do?'

'Nothing bad.' She'd done worse... 'If it works out I'll see if I can get him interested in taking a course, getting some qualifications.'

'And if it doesn't?'

'It'll keep him off the streets. Get him out of his mother's hair for a few weeks.'

'You like to live dangerously, don't you?'

'Wayne isn't dangerous. He isn't even bad.' He just needed someone to give him a chance.

Dominic walked around the car, climbed in beside her and fitted the key into the ignition without saying a word. She looked at him and then rather wished she hadn't.

This was dangerous. And she wasn't talking about the sports car. She'd been doing her level best not to think about Dominic Ravenscar. The tingling.

Confined with him in the soft luxury of his car brought it all rushing back and, like anything kept under pressure, it seemed to have grown in power. Suddenly all she could think about was him. The way his mouth had felt against hers: that moment she'd turned and seen him wrapped in nothing but a towel: the way his skin had felt beneath her fingers as she'd reached out and touched his hand.

Suffocating with a raw desire that had no place in this relationship, she looked away before he could read it in her face. 'Honestly,' she said, forcing herself to concentrate on reality. 'He's a good kid. He just needs a break. Like the rest of us.'

He fastened the seat belt, started the car, pulled out into the street. Then said, 'The way the Hallams gave you yours?'

She stilled. What had he heard? Who had he been talking to? Too late to turn down his lift now... 'I didn't take you for a gossip, Mr Ravenscar.'

'I'm not. But people will talk.'

She frowned. 'Dorothy?'

'I have to thank you for sending her to me,' he said, neither confirming nor denying that she was the source of whatever gossip he'd heard. Not that it mattered. There was nothing secret about her history. The whole village knew what had happened. Most of it, anyway. At least Dorothy would be kind. 'She's rather wonderful—'

'You're very lucky to get her. She only works when she wants to these days.' When the job appealed to her.

'—although she does have a curious addiction to pot-pourri,' he added.

Oh...chickweed! He'd noticed. Could he possibly have guessed that the bergamot-scented pot-pourri was the result of all that lateral thinking?

'For moths, I expect,' she cut in quickly. 'To get rid of them, not because they like it.' Then, because she was just digging a hole with her mouth, 'I hope you haven't offended her by throwing it away.'

'No, I try to restrict myself to offending one woman at a time. She's really done a terrific job getting the house looking and smelling the way it—' he faltered momentarily '—the way it should.'

'She's a terrific woman,' Kay agreed. 'She just has to walk into a room with a duster and it instantly surrenders.' Then, 'You, I hear, aren't having the same success.' He glanced at her. It was a guess. He might, after all, have taken his rubbish to be recycled. Sara's clothes to a charity shop. She didn't think so. 'The house is clean,' she persisted, 'but the cupboards remain untouched?' Then, 'People *will* talk.'

'Not Dorothy. She's the soul of discretion. No matter how much I pressed her on the subject of Polly's father, all she'd talk about was the pub quiz championship. And how she and her team were going to win it again this year.'

She looked at him then, couldn't help herself. But he was concentrating on the road and somehow she managed a shrug. 'OK, so I was guessing.'

'And of course you were right, but what do you do with the clothes worn by someone you loved? Bundle them up in a plastic sack and give them to whoever knocks on the door collecting for a jumble sale? To be picked over, dropped on the floor, trodden on in the scrum...' He dropped a gear, pulled out and overtook a truck. 'Come on. That's got to be easy for a quiz queen who wiped the floor with the opposition the other night.'

'I'm sorry.' She felt dreadful. She would keep forcing him to confront the issue but what did she know about what he was feeling? 'I've never had to deal with anything like that. It must be difficult.'

'Difficult. That's a good word.'

And it occurred to her that she offered him an opening and instead of instantly changing the subject, he'd taken it. For a moment she held her breath, waited...

'Which bank are you going to?'

She curbed her disappointment. He'd taken the first step. She could be patient, she told herself, before telling him where she was going, guiding him through the new one-way system until he pulled up at the front entrance. Before she had even got her seat belt unclipped and gathered her belongings, he had opened the passenger door and was offering her a hand.

She was torn. She already knew exactly how disturbing it was to touch him. On the other hand, it needed practice to get out of a seat that was almost at pavement level, especially wearing high heels; something she lacked. But then she'd been busy doing other things with her life.

While she dithered he took her hand, and with one easy movement he deposited her on the pavement with her dignity intact. He clearly knew exactly what he was doing and it occurred to her that he hadn't always been a grieving widower. That he hadn't been a husband for any length of time—

'Where shall I meet you?' he asked.

He hadn't let go of her hand.

She swallowed. This was not good preparation for a discussion about a business loan. She needed to be calm, focused. OK, so she was focused—but not on the right thing. She even considered telling him not to wait. That she'd get the bus back so that she could clear her mind...

She thought better of it. This wasn't about her. It was about him. Maybe he'd talk some more.

And anyway, if he wouldn't let her drive herself in her old van, he wasn't going to stand for any nonsense about a bus.

'There's a café in the craft centre round the corner,' she suggested.

'I know it. Will an hour be enough?'

'Good grief, I hope so. I don't know enough to keep the small-business loans adviser occupied for more than ten minutes.'

'Well, let's hope he—'

'She.'

'—she knows enough to keep you occupied for longer than that or you're both in trouble. Take your time. I'll wait.' And before he released her hand, he bent and kissed her cheek. It was like a shot of electricity fizzing through her. His chin grazed her skin. The scent of him was a heady blend of leather and tweed and citrus, sending out the kind of signals that her body recognised and responded to with a speed that left her breathless, pinning her to the pavement. He didn't notice anything odd, however, didn't feel what she was feeling because he stepped back without lingering and said, somewhat brusquely, 'Good luck, Miss Lovell.'

Her own mouth did its best to form the reply, 'Thank you, Mr Ravenscar.' No sound emerged.

Dominic watched her mount the steps of the bank. She looked different with her hair sleeked up, wearing restrained make-up and the kind of simple black suit that women kept for this kind of occasion. A don't-mess-with-me suit. The kind that made them look as if they were in control of their world and if you didn't watch out might just take over yours.

And as if that hadn't been enough, she was wearing high, high heels.

Sexy as hell.

His only argument was with her hair. He preferred it mussed…the way she usually wore it. When his lips had brushed the softness of her cheek, her scent—fresh, flowery with an underlying sensuality that hadn't come out of a bottle—had grabbed at him, twisting his gut, and he'd been tempted to pull the pins and see it fall.

Not that she needed make-up. Or scent.

If he was honest with himself, he thought she looked pretty damn sexy wearing nothing on her skin but sun block, clothes that looked as if they were charity-shop cast-offs and smelling of nothing but fresh air and sunshine. Which was one of the reasons he'd been staying pretty much out of the way since the summer-house incident. At least while she was in the garden.

He hadn't been able to stay out of the village shop on the mornings he knew she'd be working, though. Not that he'd admitted, even to himself, the reason for crossing the green to buy milk or bread he didn't actually need since Dorothy had taken charge of stocking his fridge.

And somehow he'd found himself in the pub after Dorothy had been telling him about the quiz night. Just to buy Jim Bates that pint he owed him.

He'd very nearly gone to the school Autumn Fayre, too. But he'd been waylaid by the head teacher and found himself promising a donation to the school fund just to escape.

Then today, when he'd gone to post some letters and she hadn't been behind the post-office counter, or even serving in the shop, he'd been forced to stop fooling himself. Admit that he couldn't stop thinking about her. Maybe that was why he was finding it so difficult to deal with Sara's things.

He was paralysed with guilt.

Not that guilt had stopped him from opening the door when those brochures started dropping onto the mat. When he'd seen what they were, he'd known it couldn't be anyone else, but he'd opened it anyway, expecting to see her in her usual scruffy combination of hard-worn trousers, topped by one of the giveaway T-shirts advertising some new line of biscuits or coffee or baked beans that she favoured—she was obviously a favourite with the salesmen who visited the shop—and her hair tied back with one of her daughter's ribbons. Appealing enough, but when he saw her dressed to take on the world, he'd been knocked sideways. Said the first stupid thing that came into his head. That he'd been coming into town.

He just couldn't bear to let her drive away from him.

Then, somehow, he'd found himself talking about Sara when all he wanted to do was talk about her...

A traffic warden patrolling the street bent down and looked in at him. 'I wouldn't stay here, sir, unless you want to be clamped.'

Kay flung the folder she was carrying onto the table and herself into a chair opposite Dominic before he had time to get to his feet. 'Well, that was a morning that could have been used more productively double digging my vegetable garden.'

'Coffee? Tea?' he enquired, without comment, turning to summon the waitress with a glance. Why was it only men that could do that?

She looked at Dominic. At his eyes, no longer slate hard, but like silver velvet, at the thick, over-long hair he'd raked back with his fingers, his lean and hungry take-me-home-and-feed-me features. And told herself not to be so stupid.

'Make that coffee with hazelnut syrup and whipped cream,' she said. 'And I'll have a double portion of Death by Chocolate...' Oh, slug bait! Of all the chocolate cake in all the world she had to choose that one.

'Why don't you shoot me now?' she invited. 'Put me and my big mouth out of our misery.'

'I think I'd be happier if you just had a double portion of whipped cream with the chocolate cake. It'll take longer to kill you, but you'll enjoy it more.'

'I'm really sorry.'

'Don't be. And please don't start getting tactful, or thinking twice before you choose your comfort food. I couldn't stand it.'

'No?'

'No.' Then he grinned. 'Do you really want a *double* portion?'

She glanced at him. Found herself laughing in spite of the hideous hour she'd spent closeted with a woman who not only didn't possess a sense of humour, but also clearly thought one would be a dangerous liability in business.

'You're just scared I'll be sick in your lovely new car.'

'Forget the car. I don't want your arteries on my conscience.'

'It's OK. I didn't mean it. If I ate that the buttons would burst on this skirt. And it's not mine. Black coffee will do just fine.' He looked unconvinced. 'Honestly.'

He nodded to the waitress and then said, 'It didn't go well, I take it?'

'You have a talent for understatement. I even went to the trouble of borrowing this suit from Amy.' She looked down at it. 'It's one that she wears to board meetings. But was that—' she stopped, made herself think twice before she said the words that were hovering on the tip of her tongue '—*small*-business advisor impressed?'

'*I'm* impressed,' he said.

'Really?' She thought that might just make up for the rest of the morning. 'Well, that's very kind of you, but Ms Harding clearly didn't know her Armani from…from…'

'Her aspidistra?'

'Hey, I'm the one who makes the bad jokes around here.'

'Sorry. I thought I'd help you out. Since you're trying to give it up.' He held up his hands in a gesture of surrender as she glared at him. 'So, tell me. What happened?'

'She wasn't in the slightest bit impressed with my business plan, which I'll have you know I'd slaved over.'

'Can I see it?'

She indicated the folder she'd dropped on the table. 'Forget my skills, my training, the fact that I'm suddenly getting enquiries for more work than I can handle without some help. All she seemed to be interested in was my "collateral". I very quickly got the message that, since I don't own my own home, and I haven't got any tangible assets for them to grab should my "expectations prove over-ambitious"—' she made little quote marks with her fingers '—they won't be exactly panting to lend me money.'

He looked up from the plan.

'Did she actually turn you down?'

'To my face? Oh, please. She used the standard get-out of having to talk it over with her colleagues. Said I'd get their formal answer in due course. I told her not to bother. That I'd caused quite enough ecological damage to the planet filling in all her wretched application forms, producing the business plan, without having any more trees on my conscience.'

'Just because she seemed unsympathetic, Kay, doesn't mean she won't lend you the money. She might just have needed someone with more authority to approve the risk since all you have to back your application is enthusiasm and grit. Believe me, if they know what they're doing they won't undervalue those.'

She groaned, dropped her head to the table and banged it a couple of times. 'I've blown it, haven't I?'

'It's a steep learning curve. Try another bank.'

'What's the point? It's my own fault. I've been messing about, hanging on to the safety bar of my job at the shop instead of going for it. If I don't have wholehearted faith in my own business,' she asked, 'why should they?'

'You're going for it now.' Then, 'Wayne could use your van in the afternoons for the time being, couldn't he? You won't be needing it while you're working in my garden. That's a start.'

'Well, yes, I suppose he could.' Then, with more enthusiasm, 'And he could have it on Thursday mornings, too.'

'Thursday mornings?'

'It's pension day,' she explained. 'The post office is mobbed and they won't be able to cope...' He didn't quite manage to hide a smile. It wasn't an unkind smile, but she got the message. 'Oh, thistles! I'm never going to be a tycoon, running my own landscape gardening company, am I?'

'Do you want to be? A tycoon?'

She thought about it for a moment. 'It would be great never to have to worry about money. But that's what tycoons do, isn't it?'

'Pretty much.'

'In that case, no. Not a tycoon. I just want Polly to be secure.'

His smile faded. 'That's a fine ambition. Hold on to it.' Then, 'Maybe you'll qualify for one of those grants your legal adviser was talking about. There's a young-persons business grant, isn't there?'

'I'm not young.'

'That's a matter of opinion. I think you'll find you're young enough to qualify for one of those schemes. It might be your best bet.'

She sat back. 'You seem to know a lot about this, Mr Ravenscar. Tell me, what did you do before you took off into the wild yonder to organise vaccination programmes?'

'You've got me bang to rights, Miss Lovell. I was a business adviser.'

'Not like...' She stopped herself. 'No, forget I said that. Please. Forget I was stupid enough to think such a thing. Apart from anything else, if you were like her, you wouldn't have been able to buy Linden Lodge.'

'No.'

'Forget I even asked. It was rude. Intrusive—'

'And all a matter of public record.'

'It is?'

'All you have to do is type my name into a website search engine and press the magic button.'

She thought about it for a moment then shook her head. 'No. That would feel like snooping.'

'You think so? Someone must have been checking up on me to know exactly what I was doing. I'm sure there's been plenty of gossip over the parcels in the post office. Tons of tittle-tattle over the tea bags.'

'No...' But she blushed. 'Well, maybe just a bit. People are wondering what you're going to do, that's all. Stay. Sell...'

'And what have you told them?'

'That I'm too busy with the garden to interrogate you on your plans. Even supposing you gave me the chance. A more sensitive soul might begin to think you were avoiding me.'

'I didn't want you to think I was checking up on you.'

'You didn't want me to have another go at you about the summer house,' she countered.

'Do you always say exactly what you think?'

It was kind of him to suggest she thought before she spoke... 'I find it avoids misunderstandings. Obfuscation.'

'And how often do you get to use that word in casual conversation?' he asked. 'For that feat alone, you deserve to be enlightened.'

CHAPTER EIGHT

"Now fades the last long streak of snow,
Now burgeons every maze of quick
About the flowering squares, and thick
By ashen roots the violets blow."

Alfred, Lord Tennyson

'ENLIGHTEN away,' Kay invited.

OK, he was taking avoiding action. Again. But she'd
already put him on notice that he couldn't duck the issue
forever and she'd be lying to herself as well as to him
if she denied that she was curious about everything he'd
ever done.

Besides, talking about himself was good, surely? Even
without the benefit of couch and psychologist. Not that
he was in any hurry to enlighten her—or unburden himself.

She made no attempt to hurry him along, however,
but sipped her coffee and waited.

'I wrote a software program when I was still at university,' he began at last. 'I was broke, hungry, the over-
draft was mounting. You know how it is.' Then, perhaps
realising that she didn't, he shrugged. 'My family did
what they could, but they didn't have any cash to spare.
Basically, I was on my own.'

'You didn't fancy pulling pints at the local, or stack-
ing supermarket shelves?'

'Have you ever tried to get one of those jobs in a university town?'

Again it occurred to him that she hadn't, but she said quickly, 'Ten applicants for every job, huh?'

'And the rest. So I used what brains I had and wrote a decent little encryption program for which I was paid a few hundred pounds by a development company. It kept the wolf from the door and I was grateful for it. Then I discovered how much they were marketing it for and I thought I'd been ripped off. It was then that I discovered the agreement I'd signed for the money had given them all rights. Worldwide. Forever.'

'But that's dreadful. Couldn't you do anything?'

'No one had forced me to sign it. They'd laid the cheque on the desk and I signed without even reading the thing properly. All I could complain about was that they didn't advise me to talk to a lawyer first and why should they? It wasn't their job to do that. It was my responsibility.'

'Nevertheless it stinks.'

'Well, maybe, but the harder the lesson the faster it sticks and in the long run they did me a favour.'

'That's a very laid-back attitude.'

Maybe she looked sceptical because he said, 'There's an old saying: if someone rips you off once, shame on them—if they do it twice, shame on you. I soon discovered that I wasn't the only student who'd been turned over by a smart businessman and, since I already knew I didn't want to spend the rest of my life sitting at a VDU writing computer programs, I switched to business administration. By the time I graduated, I already had my company up and running.'

'On the basis that if you can't beat them, join them?' She wasn't impressed.

'On the basis that you can beat them. You just have to have someone looking out for you. My company was formed to protect the innocents. A one-stop shop for advice, to find capital to develop their ideas for those who wanted to do it themselves and check out the contracts for those who just wanted to sell their ideas and move on to something else.' He smiled. 'There were already people who did that, of course. They're called lawyers: daunting to a lot of young people. And expensive. My young geniuses had ideas, but no money, so I shared their risk and took my fee from a small percentage of future royalties. I slept on the office floor for the best part of a year, but even a very small percentage of millions soon begins to mount up.'

'What happened to your company when…?' She stopped.

'When Sara died and I stopped giving a damn?' he asked. Then, with a shrug, 'It's still doing its job, but my profits are channelled into a charitable trust these days.'

'You give a damn. You just don't like people to know about it. It's your charitable trust, your money financing the aid projects you've been covering, isn't it?' She didn't wait for him to answer. 'I shouldn't complain, should I? I'm well off by comparison with the people you help.'

'Yes, you are. But you're not complaining, you're chafing with frustration because you have a dream and you can't see how to make it work just now. But you won't give up. You're not a quitter.'

'You'd better believe that,' she said, a subtle reminder

that he might have changed the subject this time, but she wasn't going to let him get away with it indefinitely. A reminder to herself that she'd promised to help him. And instead he was the one going out of his way to make her feel better. 'Once I take something on, I never give up.'

'It won't be easy, Kay,' he warned, not realising that she had changed the subject…in her head, in her heart. 'The thing to remember is that when you make your dream come true, it happens for other people, too. People like Wayne who need someone like you to believe in them. Your success will bring a positive good.'

'It might have done if I hadn't made a total fool of myself.' She finished her coffee. 'Thanks for letting me whine, but I think I should go home now and do something useful.'

The compost heap had never had so much attention.

'You're too hard on yourself. Let's stay here and have lunch instead.'

'Lunch?'

'Plot a strategy for your success.' He picked up the menu from the table and read off the dishes of the day.

'They all sound great, but honestly, I can't eat a big lunch and then spend the afternoon bent double in your borders, speaking of which, if we don't go now I'm going to be…' No, no, no! She had to stop thinking about herself. She was supposed to be helping him. Good food, conversation were all part of the treatment. Something she could vouch for from personal experience.

'Going to be…?' he prompted.

'Late,' she said. Then, leaning forward conspiratorially, 'The thing is, I've got this slave-driver client,' she said. 'If I'm not there on the dot of one-fifteen to put in my two hours of toil and sweat he'll...' She stopped.

What on earth was she thinking?

'He'll what?' He was almost smiling. No, he was smiling, somewhere behind his eyes. His mouth hadn't joined in yet, that was all.

'Nothing. He's the best client I ever had. Never stands over me to make sure I'm not slacking in the borders. Never wastes good weeding time expecting me to listen to his woes and then complains that I haven't done anywhere near enough to justify the vast amount he's paying me.'

'But has this great client ever given you the afternoon off to go out to lunch?'

'What kind of businesswoman takes the afternoon off just because she's been invited out to lunch, Mr Ravenscar?'

'The kind that is being given advice for free.' He sat back. Until then she hadn't realised quite how close he'd got as he'd told his story, as she'd listened. 'You could make up the time over the weekend if it worries you. Bring Polly along and I'll watch her make daisy chains while you toil and sweat.'

She brightened. 'Well, I suppose I could do that. There's just one condition.'

'Condition? I ask you to lunch. I bend over backwards to make it easy for you to accept, even going so far as to changing our terms of engagement. And you want to impose conditions?'

'No. You're right. It's ridiculous. Out of the question. So,' she said, not pausing, leaving him no opportunity to ask what ''out of the question'' condition she had in mind. 'Lunch would be good. Something light, though. Perhaps a sandwich?'

The waitress passed them carrying a baguette filled to overflowing with crispy bacon, lettuce and tomato and with a side-serving of fries. Her gaze followed it like a hungry puppy.

When she looked back he was grinning. 'That's your idea of something light?'

'On the other hand,' she said, 'maybe pasta would be a wiser choice.'

'I'll join you.' The waitress appeared magically to take their order, and when that was done he looked at her and said, 'OK, it's your turn.'

'My turn?' She really must break herself of the habit of repeating his last words. 'My turn to do what?'

'Tell me the turning point of *your* life.' He paused for half a beat, then he said, 'What happened to Polly's father?'

Oh, great. She'd followed the trail he'd laid the way a pheasant followed brandy-soaked raisins. And she'd dropped right into the trap.

'Why do you want to know about him?'

'I don't. I want to know about you.' Dominic picked up her hand, brushed his thumb gently over her ring finger. 'Were you married to him?'

Kay laughed. The sound was shocking and she stopped immediately, shook her head. 'I'm sorry.' She used the excuse of retrieving a stray lock of hair to reclaim her hand. It was too tender a gesture… 'No, we weren't married.'

She left it at that. This was change-the-subject time. But this time he said nothing. Just sat back and waited.

She'd dreaded this moment. Had known it would

come, sooner or later, and she'd promised herself that she wouldn't run away from it again, hopeful that, if she opened up to him, told him the whole sorry story, he'd trust her enough to do the same and talk through his grief.

It meant exposing herself utterly. Was she prepared to take the risk? He might turn away from her in disgust, revulsion.

Then there'd be no more of those smiles that so rarely migrated from his eyes. But when they did... No more silly jokes. Just...nothing.

Could she bear that?

She thought about the way he'd kissed her cheek such a short while ago, wished her luck. She'd floated into the bank on a cloud of something very like euphoria. She'd never experienced it before so she couldn't be sure: all she knew was that, for a moment, anything seemed possible.

Well, she'd been shot down quickly enough. Maybe it was just her day to have her self-esteem, her dreams—and until that moment she hadn't realised just how big her dreams had been—trampled into the carpet. Maybe she should get it over with all at once.

'We weren't married,' she repeated. 'We were both still at school.' She saw his eyebrows shoot up and said quickly, 'I was eighteen.'

Only just eighteen, but long past the age of consent and certainly the only virgin in her year. Not that that was any excuse.

'I was in the sixth form,' she said. 'I was the girl who'd risen above the worst possible start in life to win a scholarship to a public school and be offered a prized place at Oxford. All I had to do was fulfil my promise, produce the right exam results the following summer. Piece of cake. I was the archetypal teacher's pet.' She pulled a face, not quite meeting his eyes as she mocked herself. 'There's another old saying, isn't there? About pride going before a fall?'

'There's no accounting for hormones,' he said, evenly. After that first startled reaction, he'd kept his expression under tight control. She hadn't the first idea what he was thinking.

'You can rely on them to let you down every time. Especially when a golden youth turns on the charm.'

She was playing with the coffee spoon, spinning it nervously in her fingers, wishing he would say something. He was good at changing the subject. She willed him to change it now.

'What was his name?'

There was to be no reprieve. All she could do was plough on. 'Alexander,' she said. 'Everyone called him Sasha, though. His grandmother was Russian.'

'A bit of a poser, then.'

Her head came up in bewilderment. Then, seeing his wry expression, she laughed. 'Have you any idea what you're saying? This boy was a god. Adonis personified.'

'I'm familiar with the type,' he said.

The laughter died. 'Yes, well, he was way out of my league. I was the class swot, the kind of girl his sort never looked at. An outsider with not a designer label to my name. No money, no "family", no Scottish estate,' she said, making quote marks to illustrate her point.

'No Scottish estate? Well, I can see that's tough.' He didn't sound sympathetic; in fact he sounded angry for some reason, and that made her mad.

'Tough? You have no idea. My mother didn't want me and, even supposing she knew who my father was, he was notable only by his absence. All I had was a series of foster mothers, some good, some average, some hateful. My only asset was my brain.' She sat back, feeling rather foolish at her outburst. Staring at the spoon, still now between her fingers. 'And even that took a day off when Sash decided to turn his charm on me.'

'I'm sorry, I didn't understand. I thought...' He let it go. It was obvious to both of them what he'd thought. That she was some precious little snob who'd looked down on her parents for not being rich like everyone else's. 'You must have been terribly lonely.'

His voice was gentle and she looked up then. Dared to face what was in his eyes. He made no attempt to hide his compassion.

And she found herself struggling against tears. Clamping her jaw down hard. Swallowing the lump in her throat.

'Yes, well,' she said, with a gesture that brushed the question of loneliness aside. 'If I'd been part of the in-group, one of those street-smart girls who were eighteen going on thirty, who watched the folly of others and dissected it for their own amusement, I'd have understood what was going on. In my innocence, it never occurred to me that he was just working his way through the girls in our year, honouring each of us in turn with an opportunity to experience his magic.'

Dominic said something under his breath, but when she looked up, waited, he shook his head.

'It was a game. They all understood that. Took it as a bit of fun, part of growing up. I thought he actually meant the things he said. Afterwards, when I told him that I was pregnant, he just sighed and said that he should have stuck to his first instincts and left well alone, but the other girls had said it wasn't fair to leave me out just because I was a geek. He was doing me a favour, for heaven's sake. He'd thought I was *bright*. Told me to deal with it.'

'Deal with it? He expected you to get rid of the baby?'

Dominic sounded as horrified as she'd been at Alexander's casual, callous attitude.

'I didn't expect him to play the loving father. I'd twigged that I'd been a complete fool when…well, almost immediately. I did expect him to act like a gentleman. I thought that all those fine school ideals—honour and decency—that were drummed into us endlessly at morning assembly actually meant something. Pathetic, isn't it?'

'What's pathetic is that he got you pregnant. Hadn't he heard of safe sex? Surely all those street-smart girls insisted on protection?'

'The condom broke. He wasn't especially bothered. I was a virgin. No danger to him…' She shook her head. 'He muttered something about seeing Matron, that she'd sort it, but I would rather have died than admit to anyone what kind of a fool I'd just made of myself. I just shut it out. Refused to admit it to myself. Unfortunately pregnancy has ways of making you take it seriously; you can't hide morning sickness when you're living in close quarters with a load of girls. When someone tipped off Matron, her complaint was not just that I'd had unprotected sex, but that I'd been too stupid to go and ask her for the morning-after pill.'

'Which fine institution *is* this?'

'Don't blame her. She was in charge of a mixed

boarding-school, full of seething hormones looking for an outlet. She was dealing with reality.'

'So what happened next? I suspect this wasn't the kind of enlightened establishment where girls are allowed to continue their education with time off to visit the local antenatal clinic.'

'What happened next was that she fixed me up with a termination at a private clinic.'

'Oh, great.'

'No, I was getting exactly the same deal as the girls whose parents paid huge fees to send their daughters to the school. No discrimination because I was a scholarship girl who'd spent her first twelve years being shunted from pillar to post. In fact, the deal was better for me. I had no parents to pay for a termination; I was getting special treatment because I was a scholarship girl, someone they'd taken off the scrap heap of life and given a chance and it had paid off, big time. I was going to bring extra kudos to the school—living proof of their altruism.'

Her mouth was dry. She hadn't talked about it for a long time, had tried not to think about it. Even now, laid out coldly like this, it still had the power to shock her. 'Do you think I could have some water?'

Dominic felt sick. He hadn't intended to dredge up painful memories just to satisfy his curiosity about some man who could apparently abandon not just a girl who'd loved him, but also his baby. He wanted to go to her, put his arms around her, tell her that he thought she was wonderful. Wished they were somewhere private so that it would be possible. All he could do was get the water she'd asked for and he didn't wait for someone to come to him, but crossed to the counter and fetched it himself.

'I'm sorry, Kay,' he said as she sipped at it. 'I didn't mean to cause you such distress.'

But it was as if she hadn't heard him. Or maybe, having begun to relive those events, she just couldn't stop.

'It was only when I refused to go through with it that I had it spelled out for me in words of one syllable. The choice was have an abortion or leave.'

'And the boy?'

'Apart from a certain amount of eyebrow-raising that this glamorous heir to an earldom had stooped to notice me, not a lot.' She managed to find a smile and it wrenched something loose inside him. He rather thought it was the wall he'd built about his heart. 'They told his family, of course, so that they were prepared to deal with the legal repercussions, such as maintenance.' Her shoulders moved in the smallest of shrugs. 'Maybe they found him a more reliable supply of condoms.'

He was good at hiding his feelings, but he must have betrayed something because she said, 'I can see that you're wondering why I'm living in a grace-and-favour house courtesy of the Hallams, instead of maintenance-funded luxury, courtesy of his lordship.'

'Something of the sort,' he admitted. Along with disbelief that even a callow boy wouldn't want to know his own child.

'I was confined to my room while they decided on the best course of action. One of the girls told me that the earl himself had arrived, was closeted with the head. I was terrified he'd apply pressure to get rid of the baby. If it was a boy…' Her voice trailed into silence, leaving him to work out the repercussions of that for himself.

'I can see that, in the fullness of time, that might have

messed up the chances of a legitimate heir succeeding
to the title. What did you do?'

'I ran.'

'Ran? Where?'

'Just ran.'

'But your education? Your place at Oxford?'

'I didn't think that Oxford would be interested in an
unmarried mother.' She shook her head. 'Maybe I was
too hard on them—I wasn't thinking terribly clearly—
and I could have gone somewhere else, I suppose, but it
would have meant the baby would have to be left with
a minder. She might even have ended up in care, if I
couldn't manage. History was already beginning to repeat itself. I wasn't going to let that happen—'

He caught her hand between his. Steadied it.

'I didn't find it hard to get temporary clerical work.
Then a social worker called on me. Someone had been
looking for me and they'd found me without any trouble
at all. She started asking me what I was going to do
when the baby was born, laid out the options. I was
bright, she said. I could go far. Maybe I should consider
having the baby adopted. And that scared me so much
that I ran again. I started to imagine that I was being
followed and I became totally paranoid that I'd be kid-
napped and that my baby would be taken from me. That
she'd be adopted by someone and I'd never be able to
find her. Or worse.' She gave a helpless little shrug. 'I
didn't dare take a job, the little money I had soon ran
out and I started sleeping on the streets. Begged to survive. Looking back, I can see how stupid I was. I'm sure
that all anyone wanted to do was help me and my baby.
But I wasn't behaving rationally.' She did something
with her mouth. It wasn't even an attempt at a smile.

She just pulled in the corners of her mouth in a little self-deprecating, who-do-I-think-I'm-kidding expression. 'I had a breakdown.'

And who could blame her?

'I wonder how your golden youth would have survived if he'd gone through your nightmare. Alone, abandoned...'

'Pregnant?' she offered. And finally her smile broke through. 'Thank you. That *is* a thought to cheer the soul.'

'You survived. Came through it. That is a thought to genuinely cheer the soul, Kay. But how on earth did you get from there to here?'

Kay looked down at his hands wrapped around hers as if to give her strength. That was all wrong. She was supposed to be helping him.

'A policeman found me after I'd gone into labour and couldn't run any more. No one realised I'd had a breakdown, of course—I was in pain and I wasn't making much sense anyway. They just cleaned me up, wheeled me into Delivery and got on with it, leaving Social Security to sort me out later. I was in bed, half asleep, my baby girl in the cot by my side, when I heard a man's voice. He was asking for the young woman who'd been brought in by the police. He asked for Katie Lovell.'

'Katie?'

'Katherine, Katie, Kay. The older I get the shorter my name becomes... Anyway. I didn't stop to find out who it was. My clothes had been taken away, but I grabbed some from the next locker along with some money. I didn't know who they belonged to, or where she'd gone, and to be honest I cared even less. I just took my baby and ran.' She shivered to think of what she'd done. How it might have ended. 'Security's tighter these days. I wouldn't have got away with a newborn baby so easily now.'

'Where—?'

Their food arrived and Dominic was forced to release her hand, sit back, be patient while the waitress organised the dishes, made sure they had everything they wanted, but he wasn't interested in food.

'Where did you go?' he asked, stunned by her courage, her determination. A few minutes ago he had been advising her to stick with her business plan. She needed no such advice from him.

'To Aunt Lucy's.' She shook her head. 'No relation. Everyone calls her that. She's fostered hundreds of children over the years. I was sent to stay with her for a week before I took up my scholarship. She organised my uniform, saw that I had a decent haircut. That I knew how to deal with the confusing array of cutlery. She was brilliant and I never forgot her kindness. I thought if I could just get the baby to her, she'd know someone who'd take her, keep her safe, adopt her even.' She shook her head. 'Suddenly my worst fear seemed like the only solution. To hide her from them.'

'And you?'

'Me? I didn't matter. Only the baby mattered.'

Her voice faltered and for a moment their gazes locked, held, and he knew they'd both stood on the edge of the same temptation. To just let go...

'I left Polly on her doorstep with a note telling her what to do. I didn't sign it. Just put my initial...'

'K.'

'It sort of stuck. Lucy didn't have a clue who I was when they finally caught up with me and I refused to answer to anything else for so long...'

'I think you've outgrown it, Kay. I think you're every inch a Katherine.' She blushed. He loved it that she could still blush. That despite everything she'd been through she could still be touched by a simple compliment. Or maybe it was because of everything she'd been through. 'So, how did they eventually find you?' he asked. 'How were you finally reunited with Polly?'

'I was miles away before it occurred to me that Lucy might not do as I asked. That she might feel she had no choice but to call Social Services and I knew, if she did that, they'd publish an appeal for the mother. That it would be in the newspapers. I tried to get back before the baby was found, but I'd been careful to ensure she was found quickly. So then I had to hang around, try and find out where she was.'

She picked up a fork, toyed with a small parcel of pasta, stirring it around in the sauce.

'And?'

'She'd done exactly as I asked and taken my baby to Amy and Jake Hallam, risking goodness knows what to do it, too. She'd fostered Jake when he was a very bad young boy.' She grinned. 'He wasn't always the darling of the financial papers.'

'Is that right?'

'They had three boys of their own, but Amy had always wanted a little girl. It was the perfect solution.'

'They couldn't just claim her as their own, Kay. Nobody can just do that. There are formalities, laws…'

'They have a lot of money. A lot of power. And a lot of love to give. I don't think anyone would have said hang on there, wait a minute, this baby can't stay in your beautiful home, with a mother and father and a nanny to make sure she never wants for anything. It's not as if there are dozens of foster places just waiting for a baby to fill them.'

'When you put it like that...'

'It wouldn't have been easy, but they could have done it. But Amy is a mother, too. She knew I was in trouble. That I needed help. That I wouldn't go far.' She blinked, looked surprised as a tear dropped into the sauce. 'She wanted a little girl of her own and she could have had mine, Dominic. But she and Jake found me and gave her back to me.' A second tear joined the first. 'Gave me back my life.'

Her hand was trembling and as the fork dropped, clattering into the dish, he was round the table to lift her from the chair, hold her, whisper soothing comfort words into her ear—words that he hadn't said in an age, words that felt rusty on his tongue—terribly afraid that he'd stirred up such bad memories that she'd get sucked in by them.

But when at last she looked up, despite the tears welling up in her eyes, she was back in control. 'I'm really sorry, Dominic, I don't think I can eat anything right now.'

'No.' His own throat was pretty well stuffed with emotional rocks, too, and, aware that they were attracting curious glances, he said, 'Let's go home...' He stopped. Home. He hadn't thought of it as that for a long time. 'I'm no cook, but I can open a couple of cans of soup.'

He was still holding her. Didn't want to let her go. But she straightened and he said, 'OK now?'

'Fine. Really.'

With no excuse to hold her, he stepped back, took out his wallet, dropped a couple of notes on the table and smiled apologetically at the waitress before opening the door and ushering Kay…Katie…Katherine into the courtyard outside.

'That was Amy's first shop,' she said as she picked her way carefully over the cobbles in her high heels.

He wanted to reach out, take her hand. But she seemed to be intent on keeping her distance, returning the conversation to the ordinary, so instead he glanced at an exquisite black and gold boutique that appeared to be overflowing with exotic oils, soaps, candles. And found his attention suddenly riveted by a display of small citrus fruits in a basket, and a sunny sign that read "Lift Your Spirits…"

And he thought about the fresh citrus scent that pervaded his home courtesy of Dorothy's pot-pourri. Thought about the fact that the three women were friends…that Katherine and Amy were much more than that. Thought about the herbs Katherine—and how quickly he'd begun to think of her as Katherine—had planted in the cracks in the paving of his terrace, softening the steps that led down into the garden. How the scents of thyme and marjoram followed him everywhere. What did *they* do to the spirit…?

'Now she has them in just about every town and city in the country,' she added, turning away. Perhaps realising that the display was something of a give-away and belatedly wishing she hadn't stopped after all.

'Maybe you'll follow in her footsteps,' he said, moving on. She glanced at him. 'Daisy roots spread, don't they? Given half a chance?'

'Like weeds,' she agreed. 'But they use solar energy, which, unlike the internal combustion engine, is free.' She stopped, clapping her hand to her mouth. 'My van!

It's still sitting outside your house with the keys in the ignition. If that's gone I'm up a well-known creek without a paddle! Where are you parked?' As she quickened her step, her heel caught in the uneven surface and she was abruptly checked.

He caught her, held her shoulders to steady her, meeting her gaze for a moment, and then he was the one who was knocked sideways. Had been from the moment he'd seen her smothered in flour and blushes. By her liveliness, a vulnerability she tried hard to hide and now by her thoughtfulness and compassion. 'Are you all right?' he asked and she nodded quickly.

'You'd better wait here. I'll go and fetch the car.' And when she would have protested, 'I'll be quicker on my own.' On his own he'd have a chance to recover from the continuous close encounters that were beginning to make rational thought nigh on impossible.

Kay looked up from the careful placement of her feet just in time to see something flutter from Dominic's pocket as, taking his car keys from his pocket, he walked quickly away.

'Dominic, wait! You've dropped...' But his long stride had already carried him out of sight. It didn't matter. It was just a stem of dried-up leaves that crumbled in her fingers. Her instinct was to sniff at the remains and she caught the faintest scent of a herb. Marjoram. He was still carrying about the sprig she'd picked and given to him?

There were any number of reasons why that might be. That he'd simply stuffed it in his pocket and forgotten about it was the most obvious one.

Except that he'd been wearing a different jacket.

CHAPTER NINE

*"Thus may we gather honey from the weed,
And make a moral of the devil himself."*
                                    William Shakespeare

KAY'S VAN was sitting in front of Linden Lodge exactly
as they'd left it, but Dominic decided that reminding her
of his assertion that no one in their right mind would
take it wouldn't be kind. Not now her business depended
upon it.

Instead he said, 'Maybe you'd better lock it before
you come in. It doesn't seem wise to mock providence.'

She seemed to hesitate, draw back a little, and he
sensed that she was about to make some excuse about
needing to go home. He wasn't giving her the chance.
Not because there were still a dozen questions burning
inside his head—she'd been through enough for one day
and they could wait—but because he knew she would
be better off occupied. Thinking about something else.

'We'll take a look at those brochures,' he said, taking
the keys from the ignition, locking the door. 'And, since
I gave up my lunch for you, you can tell me the condition you were going to impose on joining me for
lunch.'

Her hand flew to her mouth as she blushed again, not
prettily this time, but hotly, covered in embarrassment.

'Oh, no...'

She'd clearly hoped he'd forgotten. Didn't want to be

reminded of something she'd thrown out when she was confident enough to tease him. Now she was feeling vulnerable and, even as he hated himself for being the cause of such confusion, some half-forgotten instinct—something predatory, primitive, wholly male—made him press her for an answer.

'Oh, yes.' And he held on to her keys.

For a moment neither of them moved. Then she gave a studied little shrug and it occurred to him that she'd practised that gesture…used it as a way of distancing herself when she was unsure of herself. 'It wasn't anything onerous,' she said and lowered her lashes, shadowing her eyes. 'I was simply going to try for a little quid pro quo, hoping to twist your arm into agreeing to come to the harvest supper tomorrow evening.' Her mouth became soft as she offered this small temptation to leave the house, join in the community celebration, become part of the village. And he knew exactly why the golden boy had taken the trouble to seduce her.

She was vulnerable, untouched and, despite the jokes, the in-your-face style, she was painfully shy. The most difficult prey. And men were hunters by instinct.

His had been in hibernation for so long that he'd forgotten what it was to see a woman touch her bottom lip with her tongue, see the betraying flush warm her cheeks as she looked up at him before lowering her lashes—a flirtatious catch-me-if-you-can temptation when it was done deliberately; devastating when it was genuine—and this was genuine. But it was all coming back to him with breathtaking speed and he wanted to roar…

'Not with *me*,' she added, quickly. 'Everyone will be there.'

'Yes, I remember.'

The thought of joining a room full of people hell bent on having a good time filled him with dread. The thought of being there with her...

'You won't get another chance to taste my blackberry and apple pie,' she said, quickly recovering her in-your-face directness.

'Wouldn't that be *our* blackberry and apple pie?' he responded.

'Oh, yes.' Then, 'Even more reason to come.'

On the surface she seemed confident, direct, unstoppable. It was just a façade; she retreated like a snail the moment she encountered the slightest barrier and he couldn't bear to see her recoil from him. So instead of succumbing to those instincts that were driving him to reach out, touch her full lower lip with his thumb, taste it, he said, 'I promise I'll think about it.'

He'd think about it. He'd think about how it would feel to sit pressed up alongside her on the long benches set up to trestle tables groaning with food, wine, beer, fruit juice for the children. Have her look up at him, see the laughter die in her eyes. Her lips full and soft a sweet invitation. How it would feel to put his arm around her, how her waist would feel beneath his hand.

He was rather afraid that he wouldn't be able to stop himself from thinking about it.

'But only if you'll come in now and have something to eat,' he added, briskly. 'And when you've given me the benefit of your advice on the summer house, I'll give you the benefit of mine on your business plan.' He held out his hand. 'Is that a deal, Katherine?'

'It's a deal, Mr Ravenscar.'

'Dominic.'

Her hesitation was infinitesimal. 'It's a deal, Dominic.'

Even as she said the words, she knew that she should not be doing this. She'd wanted to help him and maybe she had, a little, but it felt a lot safer with him calling her Miss Lovell: when she'd been calling him Mr Ravenscar. There was a safety in irony. Or maybe that was just as much an illusion as his first glimpse of her. The formality had, after all, been nothing more than a game…and all games involving men and women were dangerous.

He could make ''Miss Lovell'' sound like a caress while his name filling her mouth was sensuous, exciting, fraught with the kind of risk that could get a girl into all kinds of trouble.

He continued to hold her hand as she walked up the steps and into his house.

Katherine. The name continued to resonate in her head.

No one, in all her life, had ever bothered to call her by her full name. It made her feel special, cared for— which was strange; she'd set out to rescue Dominic Ravenscar from the past, but in the last hour the roles had somehow become reversed and now he was rescuing her.

Or maybe they were just rescuing each other.

'Mummy, am I going to have a party?' Kay pushed open the gardener's gate at Linden Lodge the following morning and Polly skipped ahead of her as she closed it and bolted it behind her.

'A party? Why would you have a party?' she teased.

'Oh, you *know*. It's my birthday. In *two weeks*! I have

to have a party. At the village hall so that everyone can come.'

'Does that include me?'

She came to an abrupt halt as she saw Dominic sitting on the lawn, using a sharp knife to cut away the grass that had grown over the stepping-stone path. A job she was leaving until the weather changed and it was too wet to go heavy-footing it through the borders. He didn't stand up and he didn't look at her, only at Polly.

They'd spent the previous afternoon sitting at the kitchen table, eating the sandwiches Dominic made for them, looking at summer-house brochures, talking about the places he'd travelled to, the things he'd seen, both dreadful and wonderful. Wondering at the power of the human spirit to endure. Until finally they'd both fallen silent and only the delicate chiming of a clock had reminded her that she had to go and fetch Polly from school.

Polly looked at him now, a doubtful expression creasing her brow. 'I don't know,' she said. 'It's for little kids.'

'You're not little.'

Kay bit her lip. It hadn't occurred to her that he would be good with children, but why wouldn't he be? He'd been good with her. A great listener. He knew the moment to prompt, the moment to stay quiet, the moment to change the subject. If only she could get him to talk.

'I'm the tallest girl in my class,' Polly said, then with a huge sigh, 'Mummy says I'm growing like a weed.'

'Really? What kind of weed. A daisy?'

'Daisies aren't big. Look...' She dropped her bag of toys, plopped herself down beside him and began picking the daisies that were spouting freely now that the grass had been cut. Something Kay mentally made a note to do something about. Perfect gardens did not have daisy-strewn lawns. Cheerful gardens did, though. 'See?' Polly said, holding one up. 'It's really little.'

'A dandelion, then?'

She giggled.

'No? What about a thistle?'

'Maybe…' She glanced up. 'Are thistles weeds, Mummy, or wild flowers?'

'It depends where they're growing,' Kay replied, with considerable feeling. 'Can I leave you to continue this fascinating conversation with Mr Ravenscar while I start work?'

Polly glanced at him, then shrugged and said, 'OK. Can you make daisy chains, Mr…?' She hesitated as she tried to get her tongue around his name.

'My friends call me Dom,' he said.

'Dom? That's not a proper name.'

'It's short for Dominic.'

'Oh, right. There's a boy called Dominic in my class. He is *such* a pain. Now, then, this is how you make a daisy chain.' She looked at him to make sure he was watching, then held up the daisy stalk so that he could see what she was doing.

Kay held her breath. Dominic had offered to keep an eye on Polly, not join in her games or listen to her incessant chatter.

'So,' he said, picking a couple of daisies and having a go himself, 'tell me about this party…'

It was a perfect afternoon. She cleared a huge section of the border with the sun on her back, all the time listening to Dom's soft voice as he teased her daughter and Polly's giggles and non-stop chatter.

Blissful.

'Hey, time's up!' He passed her a mug of tea as she straightened and pulled the rubber gloves from her hands. 'It's looking good.'

'Thanks. And thanks for clearing the paving stones.'

'I could hardly lie back in a deckchair while you slaved away, and actually I enjoyed it. I never seemed to have the time…' He shrugged. 'I was always too busy.'

He said the words as if he'd suddenly realised what he'd been missing—as if he was seeing his past instead of the present. And she felt the ground shift dangerously beneath her feet. 'I'll cut the grass on Monday so you can see how good it's going to look,' she said, briskly. 'And I'll think about some kind of feed and weed for the lawn. Deal with the daisies.'

'Leave it to me. Cutting the grass, that is. I'll leave the technical stuff to you.' He looked around. 'Although I do think daisies give a lawn character, don't you?'

'In moderation,' she agreed.

He glanced back at her. 'Unless you think I'm being cheap? Trying to save myself some money?'

'Oh, please. You're welcome. There's enough work here for everyone and I hate cutting grass.' And he looked so much better for an afternoon in the sun. Which was ridiculous. He wasn't pale, far from it. He had the weathered complexion of a man who'd spent a lot of time in the last few years out of doors in a hot climate. But he did look…different. More relaxed. There was nothing forced about the smile… 'Thanks for putting up with Polly.'

'She's a great kid. Terrific imagination. I had no idea that dolls lead such full lives,' he said, watching her gather up her toys, talking to them all the time she was putting them away in her bag. 'She's a real credit to you.' He looked as if he was going to say more, but then said, 'She's given me the low-down on every child in her class at school. *And* the teachers.'

Kay grinned. 'The parents have a deal with the teachers…if they don't believe everything they hear about us, we won't believe everything we hear about them.' Then, suddenly self-conscious, 'I have to go…'

'I'm sorry, I'm stopping you from getting ready for the harvest supper.'

'That isn't going to take long,' she said, following her daughter's example and gathering her tools. 'The pies are defrosting in the pantry—all I have to do is put them in the oven. And make a gallon of custard.'

'Do you need a hand to get it all over to the village hall?'

She turned, looked at him, not quite believing what she was hearing.

'I thought about it,' he said.

'Well, thanks. That would be great. Why don't you come over to the cottage at about five-thirty?'

Kay hadn't planned on going for glamour—the harvest supper wasn't that kind of evening, especially when you were helping to serve the food. But she used her ''for best'' shower gel that Amy had given her—the one with ylang ylang and rose otto and pure orange oils: took a little more time than usual over her hair: used some colourless varnish to add shine to her nails. And since a certain amount of effort was expected for a village event, even when she would be covering it up with an apron for most of the time, she decided to wear a peasant

blouse and a print skirt, instead of her usual trousers and
T-shirt.

She looked at her reflection in the long mirror behind
the door and was momentarily taken aback by her own
appearance. She'd dressed up for the bank, but that was
different. She'd looked businesslike. Focused. Now, with
her hair loose, her shoulders bare, her ankles emphasised
by spiky high-heeled sandals, she looked like a girl
about to meet a man she was ready to fall in love with.

And she groaned.

How obvious could she get? The entire village would
take one look at her and know. Amy would know.
Worse…Dominic would know.

She tore off the blouse, quickly replacing it with a
plain turquoise T-shirt which more or less toned with the
skirt. It didn't have an advertisement for dog biscuits on
the front, but it didn't scream ''come and get me'', either. That peasant blouse would definitely go into the
next jumble-sale bag.

Come to think of it, that was where she'd bought it…

And what on earth was she thinking of with those high
heels? She kicked them off, dug out some flat ballet-
style pumps, tied her hair back.

She was still weaving Polly's hair into a braid when
there was a tap at the back door. 'It's open,' she called,
glad to have something to concentrate on as it opened
and the coppery evening sunlight spilled into the hallway.

'Am I too early?'

She glanced up as Dominic spoke. He filled the doorway, a dark silhouette, all wide shoulders and long legs;
without warning, her fingers were all thumbs and she
had to pull them back into her palms. Polly took it as a

signal that she was done and dived to welcome their visitor.

'Dominic,' she said, taking his hand and dragging him in. 'The dolls have had a meeting with the teddies and they've decided you should be invited to my party.'

'Polly!' She pulled a face to cover her embarrassment. 'I'm sorry, Dominic—'

'If you'd like to?' Polly added, not moving, and with a shock she heard the plea in her daughter's voice. Recognised a danger she hadn't anticipated.

Dominic yearned for his dead wife.

Polly yearned for a father.

As for her…

'Polly! Hair. Now!'

'Shall I start moving things?' Dominic asked.

'Oh, yes. Thanks. If you could take one of the covered trays from the kitchen. Be careful. The dishes are hot. You'll find Dorothy and Jane Hilliard in the village hall. They're in charge and they'll tell you where to put it.'

'OK. I'll be right back. We'll discuss that party invitation later, Polly,' he said, giving her a wink as he disappeared into the kitchen.

And her heart didn't know whether to soar or sink.

'Come on, weed,' she said. 'Let's finish your hair.' But Polly wouldn't leave the house without the daisy-chain crown that Dominic had made for her.

She spent the first half of the evening torn between keeping her distance from Dominic to protect herself—and Polly—from wanting more than he could possibly give them, and staying close enough to guard him from the attentions of curious villagers.

But he seemed to be holding his own, renewing old

acquaintances, talking quietly to people, and after a while she relaxed a little. It was ridiculous to be so protective of him. He was a grown man. He'd lived in a harsh world for the last six years. He didn't need her to guard him. On the contrary. He scarcely seemed aware that she was in the same room.

'Kay, I've been looking everywhere for you. I'm taking the children home now and Mark asked if Polly can come with us for a sleep-over.' She'd been avoiding Amy, too, but now she'd been run to earth in the kitchen, where she'd been hiding out, scraping a pile of plates ready for the dishwasher and trying to sort out her feelings. 'Are you happy with that?'

Surprised that Amy was being quite so meticulous about asking, rather than telling, she said, 'Oh, well, yes. If it's not a nuisance.'

'Polly is never a nuisance.' Then, 'Good grief, what on earth are you doing?' Amy said, not ducking away as they'd both been doing for the last couple of weeks, but coming into the kitchen.

'Just doing my bit towards the clearing up.'

'Well, don't. There's a rota for chores and you're definitely not down for this.' Amy tapped the list on the wall and she was right. Her name wasn't on it.

'But I always—'

'No buts. You're a hard-working member of this community. You deserve to enjoy yourself for once. Get out of here and let your hair down, have some fun with the grown-ups.'

'I am. Really. Having fun.'

'Oh, right. Good-looking man out there being mobbed by every woman under the age of fifty whose husband hasn't got her on a tight leash. You in here, scraping plates.' She balanced her hands as if weighing the choices. 'No, sorry, it doesn't work for me.'

'He doesn't need me to hold his hand, Amy. He's doing fine.'

'He came with you.'

'Correction, he helped me carry across the pies. He hasn't looked at me all evening.'

'While you've spent the entire evening gazing pitifully at him, I suppose. You can tell almost as much from which couples aren't exchanging glances as those who are. Sometimes more…'

And somehow she was in Amy's arms. 'I'm sorry. I'm so sorry. I should have listened to you, you're always right.'

'I was spectacularly right about you,' she said, gentling her as she would a child. 'Taking the risk when everyone said I was crazy. But I was wrong to keep you so close, not to encourage you when you wanted to stretch your wings. And I was wrong about Dominic Ravenscar, too. I should have had more faith in you and for that I'm the one who's sorry.'

'I haven't done anything. Just talked to him.' Kay wiped away a tear that had squeezed from beneath her lids, found a smile. 'Even when he didn't want me to.'

'The way I talked to you.'

'And got rid of a heap of weeds. Let in a little light to give the plants a chance to grow.'

'Maybe that's all that was needed. The thing is you saw what was needed and you weren't afraid to confront the problem, do the hard work. He looks a different man from the wreck who arrived home. Jake called on him and he was shocked, really shocked at how terrible he looked.'

'Not *that* terrible,' Kay said, remembering her first, heart-jangling sight of him. Then, realising what a give-away *that* was, 'Of course, I never saw him when he was happy. When his life was perfect.' Only a photo-graph of him smiling at the person holding the camera.

'No one's life is ever perfect, Kay. Satisfaction is not guaranteed. If it was, there'd be nothing to strive for. We'd all still be living happily in caves. He needed to know that life can be good again. I saw him looking at you tonight, when you were busy. He's halfway there.'

'But Polly—'

'Likes him. I know. She told me all about her morn-ing.'

'I'm afraid, Amy. I'm afraid I care too much. I'm afraid Polly likes him too much.'

'I was afraid, too. I was certain that you'd be hurt. That you wouldn't be able to cope when you were. I'm even more afraid that because I've been over-protective, selfishly keeping you close instead of letting you fly free in case you take Polly away, that you'll back off from the risk. And be hurt anyway.'

'You've done nothing wrong, Amy. I'm the one who's spent my entire adult life running away. I've only realised, since I met Dominic, that I'm still running…'

'Then you've both learned something useful. Now it's time to go and put the knowledge to practical use. And since you're both bright and will probably reach ad-vanced level very quickly,' she said, 'you might find a use for these.'

By the time Kay had opened her hand and realised what she was holding, Amy had gone.

She found Polly, kissed her. Stood in the doorway waving her off with Amy and the boys. Tempted to just keep walking herself. Go home. Forget all about her determination to stop running.

Easy to say, but she knew, just knew that all eyes would be on her as she made her way across the hall to where Dominic was sitting with Jake, the Hilliards, the vicar. Everyone would know what was burning a hole in her pocket.

''Scarlet Woman'' would be branded across her forehead…

'I thought you were leaving without me.'

She spun around and discovered that she didn't have to make that long, exposed walk across the village hall. That Dominic was at her side.

'No…' she said. 'I wasn't planning to desert you. I was just waving Polly goodbye. She's sleeping over with the Hallams. She and Mark are best pals. It's understandable. She spent her first year in the same nursery as him.' Then, 'Have you had enough?'

'I've had enough of talking. I thought you'd never take off that wretched apron so that I could ask you to dance with me.'

'Dance?' She hadn't expected him to want to dance. It seemed a rather public display for such a private man. 'You don't have to. Really.'

'Are you turning me down, Katherine?'

She looked beyond him into the hall. The music, which had been a lively toe-tapping mixture to keep the youngsters happy, had suddenly become slower, smoochier. People were dancing up close and she thought about him holding her like that. The touch of his shirt against her cheek, the feel of his hard body against hers. Thought about how she'd been running all her life. And how good it would be to stop, come to rest in his arms.

'No, it's just…'

'Just?'

Feeling foolish, she said, 'I've never actually done this. Danced like this with a man.'

'Are all the men in Upper Haughton blind?'

She blushed. 'I'm usually in the kitchen most of the time. And then I have to get home for Polly. I think someone must have messed up with the rota…' And Amy had taken Polly home.

His smile was a curious mixture of pleasure and regret. 'Well, it's been a long time since I've done this, too, so we'll just have to help each other out. You put your hand here.' He took her hand, lifted it to his shoulder, held it there for a moment, only letting go when he was certain she'd leave it there. 'And if memory serves me, I put my hand here.' His palm nestled at her waist, his fingertips brushing lightly against her spine. She shivered. 'Have I got it right so far?'

'It, um, feels right.' The words came out as little more than a mumble through lips that no longer seemed to be under her control.

Then, 'It helps if you get a little closer.'

She blinked, made an effort to concentrate on what he was saying, rather than how good his mouth looked saying it, and moved an inch or two nearer to him.

'Closer,' he said, not moving, but leaving her to make the move. She managed another inch. There was still clear space between them, but even so it felt like sin.

'I didn't realise people still danced like this.'

'Anything else is just exercise to music,' he said, taking her hand in his, tucking it up against his chest. 'Now we move.' Since they were standing in the doorway, Kay moved forward, in the direction of the dance floor.

Dominic stayed where he was and the space between them no longer existed. 'I'm the man,' he said, as if she hadn't noticed, 'I decide which way.' And, moving his hand from the curve to her waist, to the hollow of her back, locking them together, he eased her out of the hall and onto the paved terrace where they were on their own. 'It's less crowded out here,' he said.

It sounded reasonable…

The music was something slow and romantic, and under the deepening twilight he continued to hold her close, moulding his body to hers as they moved, very slowly, in time to the music, for a while saying nothing.

'Katherine…' He stopped and she looked up. 'The pie was great.'

'Thank you.'

And this time, when he moved again, she lowered her cheek to his shoulder.

The music became fainter. It was grass beneath their feet now instead of concrete.

'The vicar asked me to give a talk to the Mothers' Union on famine relief. When I gave him the donation I promised.'

She smiled into his shirt. 'You could probably buy him off with a bigger cheque.'

He stopped again, looked down at her. 'No!'

It was darker away from the lights of the hall and his expression more difficult to read. But he sounded amused.

'Really. It's a well-known ruse. I should have warned you. He has no shame.'

And this time when he gathered her up she seemed to melt against him. 'I'm glad you talked me into coming,' he said.

'I didn't talk you into anything.'

'No… Katherine…' This time when she looked up he said nothing, just looked at her for what seemed like an age, before he said it again. 'Katherine.'

'Yes?'

'Nothing. I just like saying it.'

And then the softest brush of his lips left hers tingling in response.

'Katherine…'

'Yes.' The word was just a ragged breath and he kissed her again with the same gentle touch but this time it seemed to vibrate through her, leaving her boneless, so that her entire body, soft and weightless, stilled; waiting for something more.

And as if he knew he let go of her hand and cradled her head, his thumb against her jaw, his fingers sliding through her hair as he tilted her head back, and this time the kiss, still infinitely gentle—framing questions; inviting rather than demanding answers—took her somewhere else. His tongue tasted her lower lip, his teeth tugged at it and heat began to seep through her, so that she longed to be touched, caressed.

And 'more' wasn't enough. Kay wanted it all and with a tiny mewl her lips parted and the silken touch of his tongue sent a flashing signal to everything that was female in her, everything she'd suppressed for so long.

This wasn't the curiosity of youth, the surrender to flattery that had been her downfall. This was something else. Something she'd read about but never dreamed was real.

And she finally understood the aching, driving need of a desire so strong that normally sane, intelligent women would risk everything for fulfilment. Risk everything to fully know a man capable of touching her heart.

'I've been waiting for this moment all evening,' he murmured as his lips brushed against her ear, her throat.

And she said, 'I've been waiting for this moment all my life.'

CHAPTER TEN

"Bring hither the pink and purple columbine,
With gillyflowers:
Bring coronation, and sops in wine,
Worn of paramours.
Strew me the ground with daffadowndillies,
And cowslips, and kingcups, and loved lillies."

Edmund Spenser

KAY WOKE in the big bed under the high-pointed eaves of her cottage. It was early, the sky was still pink from a dawn that suggested the weather was on the change and the long Indian summer was finally surrendering to the first blasts of autumn that were rattling at the windows. It felt like an omen and she shivered.

'Cold?'

She turned to find Dominic propped up on his elbow watching her and self-consciously plucked at the cover, pulling it up to her neck. 'No...'

'Sorry?'

'No.' She forgot the weather, her foolish fears. 'How could I be sorry?' She forgot her shyness, reached up and cradled his cheek in the palm of her hand. It was cold. How long had he been lying that way, watching her sleep? 'You just took my breath away, that's all. I've never done anything like this before.' Then, 'Well, obviously I've done *something* like this...' She shook her head. 'No, I was right the first time. It was nothing like this.' She hadn't slept with Alexander. Or woken with him watching her as if afraid she might disappear in a puff of smoke if he took his eyes off her for one moment. There had been no feeling. No joy. No sense afterwards that the world had changed. Even though, for her, nothing would ever be the same again. 'He didn't make love to me, with me...'

He stopped her mouth with a kiss. His lips were cold, too. Cold and sweet.

'Did anyone ever tell you that you talk too much?' he murmured as they moved from her mouth to the hollow of her throat.

'No...' Then, 'Well, not lately. I only talk too much when I'm nervous...'

'Do I make you nervous?' On the point of denying it, as he trailed his fingers over her breast she squeaked, catching her lip between her teeth. He grinned. '*That* nervous?'

'Nnnn,' she said, through a mouth that seemed, suddenly, incapable of coherent utterance as his hand moved slowly over her stomach. 'It's c-cold...' she finally managed. 'Your hand.'

'Liar. This is the cold one,' and she shrieked as he seized her legs and jerked away the pillow in one easy movement so that she was lying flat. 'Have you any idea what I've been through since the first moment I set eyes on you?' She shook her head. 'I haven't wanted to make love to a woman for so long that I thought I'd forgotten how.'

'I promise you,' she said, 'you haven't forgotten a thing.'

'No. I saw you, Katherine Lovell, trespassing in my garden and it all came back to me in a rush. An instant cure.' And this time, when he touched her, using his mouth to make a slow traverse of her body, taking the longest possible route until he reached his destination, the only sound she made was a ragged intake of breath. It seemed like forever before she breathed out again on a long sigh.

'I've met someone, Sara.' Dominic stood quietly in the bedroom that they had shared, talking to the photograph in the silver frame beside the bed. Around him the cupboards and wardrobes stood open as if her belongings would make her presence stronger.

But the scent that he'd imagined clinging to her clothes had gone. Against the brightly polished surfaces, they all just looked tired. Old. As if she'd finally abandoned them. Didn't need them any more.

He picked up the photograph. 'I'll never forget you, my love. Well, you know that, I've told you often enough. But meeting Katherine has shown me that to remember you I don't have to block out everything else. I've fallen in love with her, but you're still a part of me. Always will be. If I had died, I wouldn't have wanted you to be alone. Never to be loved again. Never to have children.'

He paused, as if waiting for an answer. Instead, there was just the thump of the gate as Katherine arrived for work.

He looked up, smiling as he saw her framed in the gateway. Filled with joy to see her there. Eager to go and join her. There was just one thing left to do...

'She's like you in so many ways,' he said. 'She has your courage, your honesty, your directness.' He discovered that he was smiling. 'She makes the most terrible jokes, Sara. Makes me laugh. I thought I'd forgotten how to. She made me want to cry, too, when I didn't think I had any tears left to shed. She's reminded me who I am. She appeared out of the morning mist and gave me the kiss of life.' He traced the soft sweep of her hair with the tip of his finger. 'She doesn't have your style, of course. Your polish. Your self-confidence. She wears the most terrible clothes, says the first thing that comes into her head without a thought for how it sounds until it's too late. The real mystery is how I could ever have mistaken her for you...' Then, 'Oh, I see. I do see. Thank you, my darling angel...'

Dominic had discreetly taken his leave before the village would be up and about, before Polly came home, but he'd returned for lunch. Stayed for tea. Allowed Polly to monopolise him while she'd cleared up. Then he'd gone home, leaving with nothing more than a kiss to her cheek and an, "I'll see you tomorrow afternoon."

Because he hadn't expected to stay, hadn't pushed to stay or gone in for a heavy goodnight kiss with Polly in the next room, she'd felt cherished. Knowing that he'd wanted her for her company as well as for a good time in bed. She smiled to herself. It had been a really good time. Night and day.

He'd called before bedtime to wish her goodnight so that she'd known she was in his thoughts. And called again early the following morning before the mad rush to get Polly off to school, just to say hello.

She hadn't been able to get the smile off her face all morning. But now, when she was going to see him, she was suddenly nervous again. How did you talk to each other when you were lovers? How was she going to deal with the fact that she worked for him? She had no experience—

The pile of wood heaped up in the kitchen garden drove all such worries from her head. The same shiver that had rippled through her when she'd woken and realised summer had turned to autumn overnight goosed her flesh with a sense of foreboding.

She'd been encouraging Dominic to clear out Sara's belongings—and Dorothy had offered to do it for him, she knew—but he'd resisted. Turned a deaf ear. To choose to do it now, so soon after they'd spent the night together, well, it just seemed wrong somehow. As if he was doing it for her, instead of because it seemed... well... right.

Not that there was any sign of him. Somehow she'd expected to find him in the garden, doing something, anything, making an excuse to be there when she arrived. Maybe this was an excuse not to be...

She forced herself to start work. Told herself that he was probably just going to burn papers. Buried her disquiet in the patient removal of a particularly stubborn clump of dock weed that had got a hold—

'Hi there.'

She was on her knees, digging carefully down to get out the whole of the tap root. Her trowel sliced through it.

'Dammit, you made me jump!'

'That's not difficult.' She looked up. 'There's this one

spot that I just have to touch…' She realised that he was grinning and she blushed. 'Ah, I see that you remember.'

'How could I ever forget?' She'd waited a lifetime. It had been worth every minute…

'I thought you'd come and say hello before you started work,' he said.

'There's a lot to do and I didn't want to disturb you. If you were busy.'

'Too late to worry about that. The disturbance is terminal… Can you bear to leave the weeds for a while? Give me a hand.'

'Oh, sure…' But as she stood up she saw the box he was carrying, the tell-tale trail of black silk hanging over the edge. Definitely not papers.

'I'm taking your advice, you see.'

'Yes.' Then, 'Are you sure you want to do this now, Dominic?'

'They're just old clothes, Katherine. How can I ask you to take me seriously, marry me, move in here if Sara's things are everywhere? If I'm still clinging to the past?' He didn't wait for an answer. 'Can you bring the rake?'

"…*marry me*…"?

She couldn't have heard that right. They barely knew one another. Marriage was out of the question. She was still coming to terms with the fact that she'd fallen into bed with him. She didn't do that.

But then neither did he…

She climbed down out of the border, followed him with the rake, watched as he hunkered down to stuff some dry paper beneath the wood, set fire to it, watch it until he was sure it had caught.

She wouldn't say a word, she decided, not one word, unless he brought up the subject again. At which point she'd…she'd…

She'd think of something. In the unlikely event that it happened. It was, after all, total madness.

'Will you watch the fire while I go and fetch another box?'

'Of course.'

As the flames grew, fanned by the chilly wind, she piled on some more wood. She wanted the fire hot so that the clothes didn't just lie there and smoulder and, in the end, it wasn't so bad. Once or twice she saw Dominic stop, look at a dress or a pair of shoes for a moment before consigning them to the flames, but it was only when he opened the last small box that he faltered.

She crouched down beside him. 'Dominic? What is it?'

He gave a long shuddering sigh and she looked down, saw the soft white teddy bear. 'She was pregnant. Sara was pregnant when she died.' He picked up the little bear. 'She was furious with me for buying this. Said it was unlucky. Tempting fate…'

'No.' Then again, 'No. Life isn't like that. Sometimes it just seems that way…' As he added the bear to the funeral pyre, he stood up. Kay felt the lump swell in her throat as it was consumed by the flames and she reached out for his hand, held it tight.

'I wanted to shout the news from the top of the church tower, but she made me promise not to tell anyone until the first three months were safely over. Then, afterwards, there seemed no point. Her family were grieving enough. How could I burden them with more sorrow?'

'Of course you couldn't. Of course not.' And as he turned to her, she held him and they both shed a few tears.

Dominic for the cruelty of fate.

Katherine because she was remembering that first time they'd met. When he'd mistaken her for Sara. The urgent way he'd asked about Polly. Wanting to know who she was.

Ghosts, she thought. He'd been seeing ghosts.

She'd been fooling herself. He hadn't got over anything. He'd simply substituted her and Polly for the family he'd lost.

Dominic Ravenscar had been ensnared by a phantom image, a place-holder for his dead wife, their unborn baby, and she had been too busy being swept off her feet by a dark stranger walking out of the morning mist and putting her hormones in a spin with a kiss to notice.

That was why he could burn Sara's things now. He didn't need them as a prop any more. He thought he had the real thing.

She'd only wanted to help, but the road to hell was paved with good intentions and all she'd done with her stupid meddling had been to make things worse. Much worse.

The little alarm clock in her pocket trilled its warning and gratefully she seized her chance to escape. To think… 'I have to go, Dominic.'

'Yes, I see.' She expected him to kiss her, braced herself, but he didn't. Just held her hand for a moment as if he would delay her, as if he knew she was running away from him. 'I'll call you. Later,' he said. Then finally, reluctantly, it seemed, he let her go.

She made a brave attempt at a smile, unable to trust herself to speak, and, not stopping to gather up her abandoned tools, she fled.

Dominic didn't want to let her go. A shiver had gone through him and he had the strongest feeling that if he let go of her hand she would never come back.

Something was wrong; he sensed it.

Burning Sara's clothes had bothered her and maybe, in retrospect, the timing had been less than perfect. But wishing he'd done it before they had spent the night together wouldn't make it so and he'd wanted her to see, to know that he'd put the past behind him. That he was committed to the future. That he wanted her to be a part of it.

But it was more than the bonfire.

There was a moment at which she'd withdrawn from him; not physically—he could still feel the warmth, the close comfort of her body against his—but where it truly mattered, inside her head. She'd been relieved when the alarm had rung. Desperate to escape.

Staring into the embers of the fire, he slowly went through the afternoon—word by word, gesture by gesture—until he pinpointed the precise moment. And understood what he'd done.

She wanted to run. It was like being eighteen again and confronted with problems that she had no way of handling. Adults who wanted to manipulate her for their own ends. But she wasn't going to run away from the mess she'd made this time. That was never the answer.

If she'd had the courage to stand up for herself, for

her unborn baby all those years ago, no one could have hurt them. She knew that now. But all the knowledge she'd had then had come out of books. She'd had no emotional back-up system, no one had ever loved her, told her that her worth was more than her name on top of a list of examination results. And so she'd hurt herself.

But Amy had shown her what love was, and being loved had made all the difference. Learning how to love in return had made all the difference.

As Polly came bursting out of school, she bent and scooped her up in a hug. She may not have helped Dominic, but he had taught her something valuable. That no amount of distance could make the problem go away. No amount of time could lessen the damage. That in the end you had to face your demons.

And he'd kept asking her about Polly's father, too. Perhaps wanting to reassure himself that his perfect, ready-made substitute family wouldn't be snatched away from him. The day would come, though, when Polly would ask the same question. Who is my daddy? And she had the right to know.

She wasn't going to run away from Dominic. She'd tell him what she was doing. Not running, but walking back into the past, strong enough now to confront the mistakes she'd made. And maybe it would help him see who Polly was. Not the child his baby might have grown to be, but another man's little girl. Once she'd done that, she would do her best to sort out the present, be ready to face the future, whatever it held.

She made Polly her tea, talked about school, listened to another hundred or so compelling reasons why she absolutely had to have her birthday party in the village hall and finally left her to draw a picture of a hedgehog for the classroom wall, while she made a telephone call.

It might have been worse. The school secretary was still the same woman who'd guarded the headmaster's study. And the momentary shocked silence was mute betrayal that she remembered Katie Lovell very well indeed. Which cut down on any need for explanations.

Ten minutes later the phone rang and she picked it up, expecting it to be the headmaster himself. But it was Polly's grandfather. She listened to him for a long time, and when he'd finished she said, 'Polly, your grandpa would like to say hello.'

'My grandpa? Have I got a grandpa? Mark hasn't got one...' She took the phone and said, 'Hello? Are you going to come to my party?'

Kay covered her mouth with her hand, blinked back tears and saw Dominic standing in the kitchen doorway.

'I did knock...' He glanced at Polly.

'She's talking to her grandfather.'

'The earl himself?'

She nodded. 'He's been waiting all this time for me to call him. Wanting me to call him. Desperate.' He'd come that day to take her home with him, to look after her. He'd had people trying to find her. Besieged hospitals at the time he knew she was due...

'And Polly's father?' he said, quietly. 'Has he been waiting, too?'

She frowned. Then, realising what he was getting at, 'Oh, no...' She shook her head. 'This wasn't about me, Dominic. It was about Polly.'

'You won't be seeing him, then.'

'No. Alexander was killed last year, Dominic. He was with a peace-keeping force somewhere…' She glanced at Polly, still chatting away as if she'd known her grandfather all her life. 'What a waste,' she said, joining Dominic in the porch. 'If I hadn't been so stupid he could have known her. She could have known him.'

'If he hadn't been so stupid,' he said. 'If all those people who were supposed to care had cared a little more. But the truth of the matter is that you were both too young, too frightened…'

Dominic wanted more than anything to hold her, offer her the same comfort that she'd given him. Instead he waited for her to sit down and then sat opposite her, just taking her hands, holding them.

'Don't be so hard on yourself, Katherine.' Then, 'What made you decide to make the call now?' He thought he knew, but wanted her to tell him.

'I needed to confront my fears. I needed to straighten things out. I should have done it sooner.'

'Regret is inevitable, I suppose. When I look back my deepest regret is the time I spent in late-night meetings when I could have been at home.'

'Time is something we all squander. If we only knew—'

He stopped her with a touch to her cheek. 'We can learn from our mistakes. Learn to value each minute as the rarest, most precious thing we have, whether it's signing a deal worth millions, or dancing in the dark with a woman who, with luck, will still be hearing the same music as you in fifty years. And never, ever taking it for granted.'

She looked up. 'Dominic, we need to talk.'

'Later. Polly needs you now. She'll have questions. But I brought some photographs for you.' He'd put the envelope on the bench beside him, and now he picked it up, handed it to her. 'Look at them when you have a minute. Then we'll talk.'

'About what?'

'The past, the future…' He wanted to wrap her in his arms as if they were chains that could bind her to him. Instead he let her go. 'Us.' And he walked quickly away from her, while he still could.

Photographs? She picked up the envelope, opened the flap and peered in. They were large, glossy photographs and she took one out. It was a fashion shot, the kind of thing she saw in Amy's glossy magazines.

'Mummy… Oh, I thought Dominic was staying.'

'Mmm…'

She'd imagined Sara Ravenscar as someone like her. Tall. Fair haired. More polished, of course. A lot more stylish. She'd seen those clothes… But still a gardener with mud beneath her fingernails and on her clothes. That garden hadn't made itself.

She couldn't have been further from the truth.

'Dominic?' Polly persisted.

'What? Oh, no, darling. Not this evening.' Probably not ever.

'Oh, right…well I'll tell him tomorrow.'

'Tell him what?'

'About grandpa. He wants to say goodbye. Who's that?''

'Sara. She was Dominic's wife.'

Sara Ravenscar had been blessed with the kind of luminescent beauty that marked her out from the crowd.

He must have found these while he'd been clearing out and... And what? Realised his mistake? Why was he showing them to her? All he had to say was..."Goodbye."

What he'd said was that they'd talk later.

'Where is she now?'

'In heaven, sweetheart.'

'Like Daddy?'

She looked up then. 'Grandpa told you?'

'Yes. He's going to send me a picture. He needs the address.'

'What? He's still on the phone? Oh, chickweed!'

She rushed into the kitchen, apologised, promised to send photographs of Polly. Anything just to get off the phone.

Then she tipped the rest of the photographs out onto the kitchen table.

She was so beautiful. Hair like liquid sunshine. Her skin polished and perfect. Long, slender limbs. It was the kind of bone-deep beauty that would have turned heads when she was eighty. When she was twenty she must have stopped the traffic...

'Did he look like Dominic?' Polly said.

'Who?'

'Daddy.'

'Oh, no. Not at all. He had fair hair, like you. Why?'

'I just thought if you're going to marry Dominic he must be like Daddy, that's all.'

'Marry him? Who said I was going to marry him?'

'Everyone at school was talking about you going to the harvest supper with him. And Amber Gregson said her mummy saw you kissing him.'

Oh, terrific...

'But maybe it doesn't matter that he isn't like my daddy, because you don't look anything like Sara, do you?'

'No, darling, I'm afraid I don't...' Then, 'Not one bit.'

Kay picked up the telephone. He answered instantly, as if he'd been waiting, but before he could say a word she said, 'Why did you think I was Sara? That first morning. In the garden.'

'A trick of the light,' he offered. 'Jet lag. A small miracle. A combination of all the above...'

'Let's explore the miracle theory.'

'That's certainly my favourite. On the other hand, if I hadn't been tired beyond thought it would have taken more than a turquoise T-shirt and a straw hat to confuse me.'

'Right.'

'In which case I wouldn't have kissed you. You wouldn't have followed me into the house. I wouldn't have been forced to apologise and it would certainly never have occurred to me to engage you as my gardener, Miss Lovell. Miss Kay...Katie...Katherine Lovell.'

'Just Katherine,' she said as a smile crept up on her.

He'd said her name as they'd danced onto the village green. Said her name before he kissed her. Said her name over and over as if he'd wanted to impress on her that he knew exactly who he was kissing...

'Not "just" Katherine,' he said. 'Uniquely Katherine. Wonderfully Katherine. Unmistakably Katherine. Perfectly Katherine. Adorably Katherine...' She turned then, knowing that he was there, in the doorway. He let the hand holding the phone drop to his side and said, 'I love you, Katherine. Marry me, Katherine.'

And Polly said, 'You see? I *told* you. Can I be bridesmaid?'

'No,' Kay said. Then, 'I can't possibly marry you.'

'Yes,' Dominic said. Then, 'Why not?'

'Well. People don't, do they? Not just like that. We've only just met.'

'But all of it has been quality time.'

'Dominic!'

He raised his eyebrows a fraction. 'Are you giving me an argument?'

She shook her head and he came a step closer. 'Marry me, Katherine.'

'I can't... I've got a business to run. A child to bring up. And what are you going to do with the rest of your life? I don't want to be married to someone who's off in the wilds of the Kalahari, or trekking through some snake-infested rainforest every five minutes. I'd never sleep for worrying—'

'You'd worry?' He took a step closer.

She swallowed, knowing that she'd just made a huge mistake. 'I'd worry about anyone...'

Another step.

'Would you marry me to keep me out of danger?'

'That's not fair!'

'I have no intention of playing fair. I'll take whatever advantage I can get. So, to recap, your objection to marrying me is that you haven't known me for long enough and that I might put myself in harm's way and cause you sleepless nights?'

'Mmm.'

'So, if I told you I was going to leave the overseas trips to someone younger, that I was going to stay at home, perhaps invest in a growing concern I've become deeply interested in, maybe—with a little help—widen my charitable interests to include young people in need of a helping hand to get them started, that would deal with one objection?'

'Are you really going to do that?'

'It's down to you.'

'Definitely not fair,' she said, beginning to wish that she hadn't been quite so quick to raise the time objection. 'How can you be so sure?' she said. 'I mean marriage?' Already knowing the answer. Because she already knew—had known from the minute she thought her heart would break. 'So soon...'

'How else do you see this relationship continuing while we wait for time to catch up with our feelings? Discreet romantic assignations with early-morning departures that would doubtless keep the village amused and in gossip for a year?'

She shook her head, finding something of great interest on the floor.

'Or would you prefer to move in with me? Or have me move in with you? What's the big difference?'

'Commitment,' she said.

'Exactly,' he said and somehow he was standing up close, her hand in his. 'Marry me, Katherine.' And this time his voice was husky with something that reached deep into her, bypassing the let's-be-sensible-about-this part of her brain and going straight for the heart.

This time she didn't argue, she didn't protest, she simply said, 'When?'

'When the new summer house is built.'

'But that might be months…' she objected. And realised that he was grinning.

'We'll choose a ring together, but meantime this is a place-holder.' He took a box from his pocket, opened it, fastened the watch to her wrist. 'Just to remind us both never to waste a second.'

'Here, this way, Polly!' The hall was filled with shrieks of childish laughter as Polly and her friends played a noisy game that involved keeping a balloon in the air, with Dominic and Jake providing encouragement and the occasional long arm from the sidelines.

'Men never grow up,' Amy said. 'There's always a little boy in there somewhere just dying to escape.'

'Great, isn't it?' They exchanged a smile. 'So, when are you going to tell me your secret?'

'Secret?' Amy replied innocently.

'You've had a smile welded to your face all day.'

'I'm a naturally happy person,' she offered. 'But maybe the fact that I'm pregnant has added something extra.'

'No! But that's wonderful.' They hugged. 'I hope it's a girl this time.'

Amy shook her head. 'I thought it was important.' She laid her hand over her waist. 'Actually, it doesn't matter a bit. We've been trying for another baby for so long that I'm just thrilled—' The balloon burst with a huge bang and the little girls all shrieked even louder.

And then, as the door opened, they all turned and fell silent as a tall, distinguished-looking man stepped into the room.

'Is this Miss Polly Lovell's birthday party?' he asked. Kay's heart stopped in her mouth as she recognised the patrician features, the way his hair grew back from his forehead... Just the way Polly's did. 'I'm not gatecrashing,' he said. 'I did receive an invitation.'

And he held up one of the children's party invitations she'd printed on the new computer she'd bought with the business loan that Ms Harding had unaccountably offered after all. It had been filled in with Polly's careful printing—"Grandpa" and "Love, Polly"—but she couldn't possibly have managed the address...

How did he know? What on earth would Dominic make of him turning up like this? Then she turned and saw him walking towards them with Polly, suddenly and unaccountably shy, in his arms. And while she struggled to find the right words...any words...he somehow covered the awkward gap with introductions and the link was made. A silent clasping of hands that said everything.

When, having regained her aplomb, Polly dragged her grandpa off to meet her best-friend-Mark and admire her presents—and Grandpa had produced a little gold locket containing a picture of her father to add to her hoard of treasure—Dominic took her hand and murmured, 'That went well. You get to meet my family next week.'

'Family?' Startled, she looked at the distinguished stranger sitting on the floor surrounded by children.

'What else?' he said. Then, 'Make sure he comes to the wedding.'

On a bright January day in a world white with frost, everyone gathered in the village church, scented with early narcissus and wintersweet, to witness the marriage of Katherine Susan Lovell to Dominic Matthew Ravenscar.

Amy was "best woman", Polly a flower girl all in yellow and white, carrying a basket filled with sprigs of white heather, rosemary and winter pansies.

Kay, in a dress of fine soft cream challis that fell to her feet, a tiny tiara to set off her hair that was, for once, completely under control, noticed none of this. All she could see was Dominic, waiting for her, his hand outstretched to take hers, hold her fast.

As Katherine's hand slid into his, Dominic felt a moment of pure joy. He'd been wandering alone in the wilderness and she had found him.

Later, alone on the terrace, looking up at the stars, Katherine said, 'I thought it would take more than a kiss to wake this garden to life. Now I'm not so sure.'

'Given with a whole heart, my love,' Dominic replied, 'a kiss can work miracles.' And in case she was in any doubt, he kissed her again.

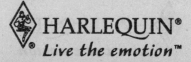

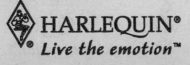

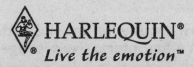

Forrester Square

LEGACIES . LIES . LOVE .

The mystery and excitement
continues in May 2004 with…

COME FLY WITH ME

by

JILL SHALVIS

Longing for a child of
her own, single day-care
owner Katherine Kinard
decides to visit a sperm
bank. But fate intervenes
en route when she meets
Alaskan pilot Nick Spencer.
He quickly offers marriage
and a ready-made family…
but what about love?

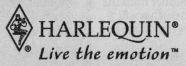

HARLEQUIN®
Live the emotion™

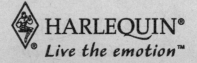

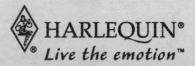